Getting personal . . .

"This is insane!" I laughed out loud. I had my doubts about actually sending a personal ad through the computer network at school, but there was no harm in at least making up the silly ad.

After thinking about it for a while, Leslie and I came up with something.

Beautiful Capricorn, 5'1", long light brown hair and chocolate brown eyes. Loves sunsets, playing saxophone, travel.

While I was trying to think of something else to add, Leslie typed another line.

Seeks fabulous date for homecoming dance. Even though it's still six weeks away, it's never too early for romance!

"I'm not so sure I like that last part," I said. "It sounds a little desperate."

"You won't get what you want unless you ask for it, Rebecca," Leslie said. She typed *send* into the keyboard, her finger poised over the Enter key.

I sat up, feeling panicky. The thought of posting my personal ad for the world to see, even though it was anonymous, made me nervous. I knew there were over a thousand kids who went to Westfield High. But what if someone figured out it was me?

"Uh . . . h-hold on," I stammered. "I don't think I want to do this. . . ."

But Leslie's finger had already hit the key. "Sorry," she said, leaning back. "It's too late!"

Don't miss any of the books in *Love Stories*
—the romantic series from Bantam Books!

It Had to Be YOU

Stephanie Doyon

BANTAM BOOKS
NEW YORK · TORONTO · LONDON · SYDNEY · AUCKLAND

RL 6, age 12 and up

IT HAD TO BE YOU
A Bantam Book / July 1996

Produced by Daniel Weiss Associates, Inc.
33 West 17th Street
New York, NY 10011

ISBN: 0-553-56669-5

Published simultaneously in the United States and Canada

Bantam Books are published by Bantam Books, a division of Bantam
Doubleday Dell Publishing Group, Inc. Its trademark, consisting of the
words "Bantam Books" and the portrayal of a rooster, is Registered in
U.S. Patent and Trademark Office and in other countries. Marca
Registrada. Bantam Books, 1540 Broadway, New York, New York 10036.

PRINTED IN THE UNITED STATES OF AMERICA

OPM   0 9 8 7 6 5 4 3 2 1

*To my parents for teaching me
to follow my heart, and to Whitney
for giving me his.*

One

"MARK MY WORDS—by the end of the first quarter, we'll both be dating gorgeous seniors," my best friend, Leslie Weaver, said as she followed me down the corridor to our fourth-period class.

I stepped carefully on the buffed floor, praying I wouldn't slip in my brand-new, stack-heeled penny loafers. "Sounds great, but I'd just settle for a date for the homecoming dance."

"We're *juniors* now, Rebecca," Leslie said. "It doesn't hurt to set your sights a little higher." Suddenly Leslie's expression became intent, and she stopped dead in her tracks. "Hold on a second."

"What's wrong?" I asked, sliding my way down the ramp and coming to a stop at the entrance to the classroom.

Leslie's lips scrunched up as if she were concentrating hard, waiting intently for something to happen. Then, out of the blue, hunky Mark

1

Pierce, star goalie of the soccer team, came barreling around the corner. We watched his perfectly muscled form zoom past us and tried not to drool.

"How do you do that?" I asked, my eyes still glued to Mark's sculpted arms.

Leslie shook her head. "It's like a sixth sense or something," she said. "Or maybe it's like radar—but lately I always know when a cute guy is around." She tossed her long dark curls over one shoulder. "It's a gift that I must use to benefit all of womankind."

I laughed. "I hate to be pessimistic, but even with a remarkable talent such as yours, I doubt either one of us could get a date with Mark. Or any other gorgeous senior, for that matter."

Leslie shrugged. "Okay, then I'll settle for an average-looking junior with a cute dog," she said as we walked into the computer lab.

There was only one available computer station, and it was at the front of the room, directly in front of Mr. Meyers's desk.

We sat down. "You can set *your* sights on a steady guy," I said, picking the lint off my cream-colored skirt with lavender flowers. "But the only thing I'm worrying about is homecoming."

Leslie squinted at me. "What's this sudden obsession with homecoming?"

Mr. Meyers glanced down at us disapprovingly through his thick eyeglasses. I ducked behind the computer and whispered to Leslie, "You remember what happened last year?"

"What? You mean Arnie?" Leslie's mouth

2

twitched at the corners, and I could tell she was trying not to laugh.

I shuddered. "It was so embarrassing. It was bad enough that he wore a purple tux that was two sizes too small, but when he started flailing on the dance floor . . ." My stomach churned from the memory. That had to have been one of the worst nights of my life.

"That's what you get for going with your aunt's accountant's son," Leslie snickered.

"But I wanted to go so badly," I said in my own defense.

"Ahem." Mr. Meyers cleared his throat loudly. "Settle down, people." When the class quieted down, he passed out photocopies of the class syllabus, lists of materials needed, and a four-page packet outlining the rules of the computer lab. More than a few students sighed heavily. We were all miserable. It was the beginning of a new school year.

While Mr. Meyers worked his way to the back of the room, I looked over at Leslie. "Why don't you come to my rehearsal tonight?" I said slyly. "Donny's going to be there."

"No, thanks." Leslie sneered in disgust.

A couple of nights a week I played with a jazz band made up of a few kids from school. I played saxophone, and Donny played drums. He had the hots for Leslie and had chased after her all the previous year. I thought Donny was really a nice guy, but Leslie thought he was too eager.

"He's a senior," I added.

Leslie shook her head. "It doesn't matter."

3

I nudged her elbow. "And he's got a really cute dog."

"His hair's too frizzy," Leslie said. "I'd rather stay home and pluck my eyebrows, thank you very much." She leaned back in her chair and folded her arms. "I want to meet someone new."

"Why don't you put an ad in the personals?" I was only joking, of course, but before I knew it, Leslie's smoky green eyes were flashing like traffic lights. Already I could see that her mind had shifted into high gear.

"Not a bad idea," she said soberly, flipping through the stacks of paper on the desk. "It just might work."

Mr. Meyers started writing notes on the chalkboard, in the same meticulous script we'd been taught in second grade. "Welcome back, everyone," he said with a little too much enthusiasm. He clapped his chalk-dust-covered hands and rubbed them together like a villain in a silent movie. "It's nice to see so many smiling and suntanned faces."

Leslie rolled her eyes. I cracked open my brand-new five-subject notebook and uncapped a ballpoint pen. Five minutes into the class, and I already had the sinking feeling that computer programming wasn't going to be my favorite subject.

Mr. Meyers smoothed back his thinning brown hair and sat on the corner of his desk. "In case you haven't heard the good news, over the summer the school board agreed to increase the budget for the computer department. Among the many changes, we have just installed an E-mail system. As of today, everyone at Westfield High has their own account."

Leslie and I looked at each other, wondering if it was some kind of weird joke. When we realized Mr. Meyers wasn't pulling a fast one on us, everyone in the class started talking at once. A few of the guys sitting in the back row made a list of all the great computer games they were going to download off the Internet.

Mr. Meyers raised his hands high in the air. "Before you get carried away, let me make one thing clear," he said. "The service is limited to E-mail between people in this school. There will be no access to outside networks."

A collective moan rippled through the class.

"But there will also be a public bulletin board where you can post messages and participate in active discussions," Mr. Meyers added excitedly.

"Bummer," Randy Potter said out loud.

Mr. Meyers wrinkled his brow and glared in Randy's direction. "Actually, I think you'll find it to be quite interesting," he said sternly. "I'm giving you the rest of the period to try it out for yourselves. The instruction sheet is in the packet I gave you. I'll be right here if you have any questions."

The class was buzzing as everyone paired off at the terminals. I turned to Leslie. "It seems kind of weird, doesn't it? Why would I want to send a letter to someone over the computer when I could write a note or talk to them face-to-face?"

Leslie was busy typing at the keyboard. In a matter of seconds, and without reading any of the papers Mr. Meyers had given us, she'd already figured out how to get into the E-mail system.

"How do you know all that stuff?" I asked.

"My mom just got hooked up at home for her job. She showed me how to use systems like this one," Leslie said. "E-mail is the coolest, Rebecca. Did you know you can send a letter to someone without them knowing who you are?"

"Oh, yeah?" I thought about all the times people had cut in front of me in the lunch line or snickered at some question I'd asked in class. Suddenly an evil fantasy popped into my head, in which I used E-mail to exact revenge on the cruel people who had done me wrong. I imagined myself sending off a slew of anonymous notes with vague, ego-damaging messages, such as *When was the last time you deep-conditioned your hair?* or *Has your grandmother been taking you shopping for clothes again?*

Leslie typed in her password, her long, frosted pink nails clicking against the keys. "On my mom's computer, you can talk to strangers halfway around the world," she said. "You have to come over and check it out sometime."

My mean streak subsided, and I looked at her skeptically. "It still doesn't seem very practical."

A list of strange words and commands scrolled up the screen. "Think of all the possibilities," Leslie said, her voice taking on an excited edge. "We can even use the computer to meet guys. All we have to do is post a personal ad." She winked at me.

"Les, you're out of control," I sighed. "Mr. Meyers said the bulletin board was for discussions. It's not a pickup joint."

"Don't be so uptight, Rebecca. This is only for fun." Leslie glared at me disapprovingly. "Besides, no one will know we're the ones doing it. My screen name's going to be Sabrina."

Without missing a beat, Leslie started typing out her own personal ad. It flowed so smoothly from her fingertips, I secretly wondered if she'd ever done something like that before.

Gorgeous Scorpio, 5'5", curly brown hair and stunning green eyes, loves action flicks, roller coasters, and moshing at concerts. Adventurous spirit with sense of humor seeks same for fun, frolic, and possible long-term relationship. No weirdos.

Leslie tapped a few keys, and in an instant the ad hurled itself through cyberspace and attached itself to the bulletin board maintained on the school's main computer. "I love technology," Leslie said with a sigh. Then she looked at me. "Okay, your turn."

In a daze, I stared at the blinking cursor on the screen. *I can't believe she did that,* I thought. Leslie had a knack for coming up with the most bizarre schemes, then making me feel like a dope for not going along. It wasn't that I didn't want to be daring; I just didn't see the point.

"Come on," Leslie coaxed. "It'll be fun."

I looked up from the computer screen. Leslie's expectant face was staring at me. "All right," I said with hesitation. I looked down at my skirt and purple sweater. "Call me Lavender."

"Lavender it is." Leslie smiled. "What do you want me to write, Lavender?"

"This is insane." I laughed out loud. I had my doubts about actually going through with it, but I figured there was no harm in just making up the stupid ad. "Start it out like yours."

We thought about it for quite a while, and finally we came up with something. Beautiful Capricorn, 5'1", with long light brown hair and chocolate brown eyes, loves sunsets, playing saxophone, travel.

While I was trying to think of something else to add, Leslie typed another couple of lines.

Seeks fabulous date for homecoming dance. Even though it's still six weeks away, it's never too early for romance!

"I'm not so sure I like that last part," I said. "It sounds a little desperate."

"You won't get what you want unless you ask for it, Rebecca," Leslie said. She pressed a few keys and then paused, her finger poised over the enter key.

I sat up, feeling a little panicky. The thought of posting my personal ad for the world to see, even though it was anonymous, made me nervous. I knew that over a thousand kids went to Westfield High. But what if someone figured out it was me?

"H-Hold on," I stammered. "I don't think I want to do this. . . ."

But Leslie's finger had already hit the key. "Sorry," she said, biting her lower lip. "It's too late."

As soon as school ended that afternoon, I grabbed my saxophone case and leather backpack and headed for Java Joe's, where my band was rehearsing. Joe's was a small café on Main Street where there were occasional poetry readings and performances by local bands. Our band wasn't quite ready yet for our own show, but the owner, Joe Mills, was nice enough to let us use his back room as a rehearsal space.

Walking the half mile to the café was a bit of a strain, since my backpack was crammed with homework assignments and books. But I didn't mind. There was something to be said for the crisp, cool air of a Maine autumn and the promise of a brand-new school year. The combination made me feel strong and invincible, as if I could do anything.

"Rebecca, it's so good to see you!" Joe greeted me with a warm hug and a smile. His smooth, round face was tanned from spending the summer at his cottage in South Harpswell. "How was your summer?"

I held one of my faintly golden arms against one of his deeply tanned ones. "Not as good as yours," I said with a laugh. "It must've been rough spending every day on the beach. I can't believe how tan you are!"

Joe scratched the top of his balding head. "The sun has nothing to do with it," he said with a chuckle. "It's all the coffee I drink." He took a sip from an oversized travel mug with the orange and blue Java Joe's logo on it. "What can I get you? Cappuccino?"

"No, thanks," I said, making a face. Nothing was grosser than a sax mouthpiece that smelled like coffee. "Just water."

"Go on in," Joe said, nodding toward the back room. "I'll bring it in to you. Everyone's here already."

I pushed open the door. Instead of being hit by

the thunderous assault of drumbeats and guitar chords, as I'd expected, the room was quiet. The equipment was still packed away, the stage bare. Instead of warming up, everyone was sitting around one of the black café tables, playing cards.

"Hey, guys," I said, shaking off my backpack.

"It looks like Synergy's main attraction has come back for another year of abuse," Donny said, staring at his cards. His frizzy red hair was standing on end. "We didn't think you'd show up."

"I wasn't going to, but I changed my mind at the last minute," I said teasingly.

Buzz, our guitar player, was wearing his usual uniform of a faded Led Zeppelin T-shirt, drab green army pants cut off at the knee, and Doc Martens. He dealt one card to each person and smacked the rest of the deck facedown on the table. "We're ready to start, Rebecca. Are you in?"

I turned a chair around and straddled it. "Actually, I was hoping we could get the rehearsal rolling."

No one paid any attention to me. Marissa, who was our keyboard player in addition to being Buzz's girlfriend, leaned over Buzz's shoulder, pointing to a card. The bassist, Andre, discarded a two of hearts and picked up a card from the stack. "Your turn, Donny," he said.

I rested my chin on the back of the chair. "Is this what you guys did all summer?"

Donny picked up the two of hearts and dropped a six of clubs in its place. "I did a few other things," he said. "Did you check out the bass drum?"

Near the stage I spotted pieces of the drum set.

The bass drum was standing on its side. Painted in black Gothic-style letters was the name of our band, Synergy. The name had been Marissa's idea—it meant the coming together of forces so that the sum of the whole was greater than its parts.

"That's so cool!" I said. "Who did it?"

Marissa smiled shyly at me and pointed to herself. She didn't like to talk unless she absolutely had to.

Joe came in with a big plastic pitcher of water and a stack of paper cups. A tall guy with thick blond hair and an oversized plaid shirt followed behind. He had a broad, muscular frame and a sweet face. I knew I had seen him in school before, but I couldn't remember when I'd seen him or who he was.

"Why's it so quiet in here?" Joe asked, setting the pitcher down on one of the tables. "I thought you guys were here to practice."

I glanced at the sound board to the side of the stage and the unlit bank of lights above. It would be tough to start rehearsal without our technical man.

"Where's Nick?" Donny asked, as if reading my mind.

Joe's forehead creased as he poured a cup of water. "Now that you're all here, there's some big news I have to tell you," he said reluctantly. "Nick quit yesterday."

"What?" My heart caught in my throat.

Joe shook his head. "He called me from Colorado," he explained. "He met some girl out there this summer and he's not coming back."

Andre's eyes lit up. "Good for him, man."

"But it stinks for us," I said. Nick knew everything there was to know about the technical side of performance, plus he knew all our songs by heart. He was like the sixth member of the group. The band was finally getting its act together, and we'd all been hoping that this would be the year we'd do a real gig. I was glad Nick had found true love in the Rocky Mountains, but at the same time I couldn't help but feel a little bit betrayed.

Buzz brushed the bangs out of his eyes. "So what are we going to do?"

"It's all been arranged," Joe said, stepping aside. He motioned for the guy in plaid to move forward. "Jordan West is going to take over for Nick. You guys know Jordan, don't you?"

Buzz and Donny nodded.

Jordan West . . . the name *was* familiar. I stole a quick glance at his dark brown eyes and cute mouth. *Why don't I remember this guy?* Then all of a sudden it hit me. His dad was Dr. Albert West, director of the music program at Bauer College, where my dad was an economics professor. It was all coming back to me. Jordan, surprisingly enough, wasn't in the school band, but spent his time fighting for tons of different causes. He was one of those annoying activist types who took twisted pleasure in telling people about the evils of everything they ate, drank, and breathed. If he would put half as much energy into working for the band as he did protesting the fur industry, Synergy would have a spectacular show.

Joe patted Jordan on the shoulder. "You know everyone, don't you?"

Jordan nodded for a moment, then looked up at me. Our eyes locked for a moment, and I held my breath as I stared into his deep brown eyes. "Except her," he said to Joe. "I don't know her." He pointed straight at me.

I exhaled slowly. Why didn't he know who I was? After all, our dads worked at the same place. We even went to the same school. A mischievous glimmer in his eye made me wonder if he was just pretending.

"I'm Rebecca Lowe." I held out my hand.

"What?" Jordan said, as if he hadn't quite caught it. He leaned toward me, and I caught a whiff of his musky scent.

"Rebecca," I answered, a little louder.

"Rebecca," Jordan repeated thoughtfully. We shook hands; his was warm. "Nice to meet you, Becky."

A strained smile stretched across my face. No one called me Becky and lived to tell about it. "It's Rebecca," I corrected.

Jordan smiled. "Right."

Joe turned on his heel and headed for the door. "Have a good rehearsal, you guys."

I turned around and opened my sax case, anxious to get rehearsal started. The warmth of Jordan's fingers lingered even as I touched the cold metal of my horn. "So, Jordan, how long have you been working the sound board?"

There was no answer. When I turned around again, I saw that Jordan had joined the card game.

Buzz studied his hand, then picked up two more cards. "As soon as this game is over, Jordan, we'll let you in on the next one."

The muscles in the back of my neck were squeezing themselves into tight knots. There were dozens of things I had to get done, and I wasn't about to waste my time watching those guys playing cards. "There isn't going to be another game," I said firmly.

They continued playing, as if I hadn't said anything at all.

Jordan looked over at Buzz's pearly white guitar, which was leaning against the amp. "Nice guitar," Jordan said. "I've always wanted a Paul Reed Smith."

Buzz nodded proudly. "Isn't she a beaut?"

My blood was beginning to boil. "Come on, guys, let's get going," I said.

Buzz ignored me. "I've got this great distortion pedal at home," he said to Jordan. "I'll bring it next time."

Jordan let out a low whistle. "That's awesome," he said.

I quickly ran through a few scales on my sax, hoping the conversation would stop before I was done with my warm-up exercises. But Buzz and Jordan were still going strong, talking about everything from twelve-string acoustics to whammy bars.

Donny threw down his hand, his face breaking into a wide grin. "Gin!" he shouted proudly.

"Oh, man . . ." Andre tossed his cards on the pile. "I'll get you on the next one." He collected the cards and started to shuffle.

I clenched my fists, anger flaring inside me. "Put the cards away," I demanded through gritted teeth.

Jordan looked at me, his brow wrinkled. "Can I ask you something, Becky?"

"What?" I snapped.

"When's our first gig?" he asked.

I looked down. "We don't exactly have one yet. . . ."

"Then what are you so uptight about?" Jordan said with a smirk. "You should learn to relax a little."

"Yeah, Rebecca," Buzz said. "Relax."

I slammed my case shut. "Let me know when you guys are serious about playing," I said, heading for the door.

"Is everybody in?" I heard Andre ask as he dealt another round.

Two

THE SECOND DAY of school was much better than the first. There was a definite, crackling energy in the air that had been seriously lacking the day before. One of the reasons for the turnaround was the anticipated arrival of that year's exchange student. According to a reliable student worker at the main office, Antonio Ramirez's flight from Salamanca, Spain, had landed safely two days earlier at the Portland airport. After a day of rest to recover from jet lag, Antonio was expected to begin his studies, effective immediately.

With the way everyone was acting, you'd have thought we were expecting royalty. Nearly all the girls at school were decked out in their most eye-catching clothes, and most of the guys had put on their coolest attitudes. No one had even met Antonio yet, and already everyone wanted to be his buddy or his boyfriend.

I was not so easily impressed.

But there were advantages to all the pageantry. First of all, there was no line in the blue and white lunchroom. While everyone else was crammed in the hallway, hoping for a chance encounter with Antonio, I was able to get my chicken salad sandwich and bag of pretzels in two minutes flat.

"Hey, you," a voice called from behind me. It was Leslie. She dropped a stack of books on the table and collapsed in a chair.

"Hey," I said, in between bites of my sandwich. "I thought you'd be out in the hallway with the rest of the free world."

"Nah. There's too much hype. This guy could turn out to be a real dweeb," Leslie said, digging into my bag of pretzels. "Besides, who has time for a foreign exchange student when I already have five dates for tonight?"

My eyes bulged. "Five? Don't tell me your E-mail scam actually worked."

"Didn't it work for you?" she asked.

"No," I said. "My mailbox was empty."

Leslie's brow creased. "That's odd."

"Not really, when you think about the ad you sent off," I said ruefully. "Making me sound desperate is a surefire way to scare off every guy in this school."

"We'll fix it," she said. "I read Meyers's papers last night and figured out how to change something on the bulletin board."

I ate another bite of my sandwich. "So tell me about your five dates."

A wicked smile crossed Leslie's face. "Well,

17

they're not exactly dates . . . ," she started.

I sensed an elaborate scheme in the works.

Leslie leaned forward confidentially. "What are you doing after school?"

I was almost afraid to answer. "Nothing. Why?"

She tugged at the sleeve of my teal blue ribbed turtleneck. "I need you to go to Bonanza Burger with me."

"Before I say yes, you have to tell me what you're up to."

Leslie looked around the empty cafeteria, as if to make sure no one was listening in on our conversation. "This is the deal," she said in a low voice. "The guys who wrote to me used their screen names, so I can't tell if they're really cool or just pretending to be. I told each of them to meet me at Bonanza Burger—at different times, of course." Leslie grabbed my arm with both hands. "While they're waiting for me, I'll be in another booth, checking them out. If I like one of them, I'll go over to the booth and reveal my true identity."

I shot her a sideways glance. "And what if you don't like any of them?"

"It's simple," Leslie said, leaning back in her chair. "I just won't show up."

I shook my head. "Les, you can't stand those poor guys up!"

"Why not?" she asked. "It's just E-mail. It's not like we even have a relationship or anything. So will you go with me?"

"All right," I said reluctantly. "But this doesn't mean I approve of what you're doing."

Leslie's face suddenly scrunched up, the way it

had the day before. "It's happening again. My radar is going off. . . ."

I looked up from my sandwich, expecting to see Mark Pierce or another one of Leslie's ongoing crushes, but was startled to see Jordan West plow through the cafeteria doors. He was wearing nearly the same clothes as the day before, except he'd changed his T-shirt from plain white to jet black. Leslie's radar was right once again. Jordan looked hot.

"Here comes the newest addition to the slacker band," I murmured as my sandwich slipped out of my hands and onto the paper plate below.

Leslie gave him a quick once-over. "Jordan's the new techie you were telling me about, right?"

Before I could answer, Jordan was at our table.

"How's it going, Becky?" he said lightly.

The card game at Java Joe's kept flashing through my mind. "It's Rebecca, and everything's okay," I grumbled.

"Glad to hear it." Jordan ran his fingers through his thick blond hair. His dark eyes dropped to the chair where I'd propped my feet. "Do you mind if I sit down?"

The table we were sitting at had eight chairs, five of which were empty, but Jordan wanted the one I had my feet on. It figured. "Go right ahead," I said, swinging my legs around.

Leslie nudged me with her elbow, indicating that I'd forgotten to properly introduce her. "Jordan, this is my friend Leslie."

"You're the new light and sound man?" Leslie asked.

Jordan waved his hand in the air. "I sure am," he

said. "Didn't we have geometry together last year? Ms. Huston's class?"

Leslie smiled. "That's right—I knew you looked familiar." She glanced at the wall clock. "It's so late! I've got to get some reading done before my next class."

I knew exactly what Leslie was up to. "You have study hall next," I said. *Don't leave me alone with him,* I begged silently.

Leslie gathered her books. "I'll see you guys later." She gave me a not-so-subtle wink. "Don't forget about our after-school date," she said before heading out the door.

"Your friend seems really nice," Jordan said, pulling his chair closer to mine.

Not knowing where to look, I studied the remnants of my chicken salad sandwich. Jordan's musky scent floated in my direction. "She's great," I said.

Jordan peered at my sandwich. "Is that tuna or chicken?"

"Chicken," I answered. "Do you want some?"

His lips curled in disgust. "No, thanks, I'm a vegetarian," he said. "Don't you know about all the cruel things they do to chickens? They stuff them in these tiny cages and—"

I held up my hand to make him stop, forcing myself to swallow the mouthful I was chewing. "Thanks for ruining my lunch," I said, pushing the plate away.

"I'm sorry, but it's nothing compared to what that poor chicken went through."

"I wish I'd said tuna instead."

Jordan's mouth turned up in a teasing grin. "Then I would've told you about all the innocent dolphins that get caught in the fishermen's nets."

"Great—now I'll never eat two of my favorite foods again." Jordan was really starting to annoy me. I grabbed my bag of pretzels and held one of them up to his face. "Do you have anything terrible to say about these? I'm sure you must have some horror stories about pretzel factories where poor little pretzels are forced to twist themselves into unnatural shapes."

Jordan grabbed the pretzel and popped it in his mouth. "No, actually, it's okay to eat these."

I bit down hard on a pretzel, feeling the satisfying crunch of it between my teeth. "What time did the card game break up last night?"

"About five, then we all went out for pizza," Jordan said. "You should've stayed—it was a blast. Or maybe you don't like having fun. I don't really know you well enough to make a judgment about that."

My jaw tensed. "Of course I like having fun," I said emphatically. "But sometimes you have to get down to business. I'm the band's leader. I'm the one who organizes rehearsals, sets up the gigs, motivates everyone. I have to maintain some sort of authority or it's useless. When no one was listening to me yesterday, I had no choice but to leave. If I had given in and stayed, I would've lost my authority."

"There are ways of getting people to do what you want without being a tyrant," Jordan said.

"I'm not a tyrant!" I answered. "Is that what you guys were saying about me when I left?"

"Not exactly." Jordan paused. "But we all kind of agreed that you're a little too uptight. Don't forget the reason you started the band in the first place—to have *fun*."

My insides felt as if they were shriveling up. Not only was I losing control over the band, but now they hated me too. Meanwhile, Jordan had just strolled in and was suddenly everyone's favorite guy.

I balled up the empty pretzel bag in my fist. "Thanks for the advice," I said in a nasty tone. "But *you* just worry about the sound board and let *me* worry about running my own band!"

"There's nothing like the smell of grease after a hard day," I said wistfully as Leslie and I walked through the saloon-style doors of Bonanza Burger. It was a tacky but festive burger joint where kids hung out after school. The theme of the restaurant was the Wild West, from the horseshoe-shaped booths right down to the miniature lassos tied around the ketchup bottles.

"How do I look?" Leslie asked me for the billionth time. She examined her dark green miniskirt in the cactus-shaped mirror.

"You look fantastic. You're going to drive those cyberguys nuts," I said, giving my own reflection a quick check.

Leslie smiled. "Only if I let them see me," she reminded me, scanning the after-school crowd.

Gary Morgan, the tallest guy in the junior class, was standing by the cash register. He was wearing denim overalls, a white T-shirt, a red handkerchief tied around his neck, and a straw cowboy hat on his head.

"Howdy, partners! Welcome to Bonanza Burger, where you don't have to be a cowpoke to enjoy a great meal!" Gary said with forced enthusiasm.

Leslie gave Gary an appraising glance. "Nice duds," she said dryly.

Gary's face fell. "I look stupid, don't I?" he whispered.

"Not at all," I reassured, reaching up to give his handkerchief a tug. "I think you look very . . . cowboylike."

"Why, thank you, Miss Rebecca," Gary said with a western twang. He grabbed a couple of menus. "Will it be two for dinner?"

Leslie nodded. "But first we need to ask you a favor."

"Shoot."

"We're expecting five friends, and when they get here, we'd like you to seat them in the corner booth." Leslie rested a hand on Gary's forearm. "The code word is *Sabrina*. If they ask for Sabrina, stick them in the corner booth—but don't mention me. Got it?"

The corners of Gary's mouth twitched thoughtfully. "The problem is, the booth only holds four people. There's no way I can get all seven of you in there."

"That's not a problem," I added. "They're coming here one at a time. Leslie and I are going to be sitting on the other side of the room."

The whole situation seemed to baffle Gary, but he was a good sport. "Sure, whatever you say. Go ahead and sit wherever you want."

Leslie chose a booth directly across from the corner booth, so we'd have a perfect view. When we finally sat down, I immediately opened the menu, starved from not having finished the lunch Jordan had ruined for me.

Leslie took a piece of notebook paper out of her purse. "This is the schedule," she said, laying it on top of the menu I was reading. "I set the dates half an hour apart, so the guys won't run into each other."

"Smart thinking." I moved the schedule off to the side to take a look at the Roundup Specials. "Unfortunately, that means we're going to be here for about three hours."

Leslie blotted her lipstick with a napkin. "It won't take that long—trust me," she said. "As soon as I hit the jackpot, you're free to go. Who knows? Maybe it'll be the first guy on my list."

A cowgirl waitress in a stonewashed denim skirt set two glasses of water on our table and pulled a notepad out of her silver and turquoise belt. "What can I get you?"

"I'll have a plate of Ranch Fries, with extra Bandit Sauce, and a large root beer," Leslie said.

I still hadn't made up my mind when the cowgirl asked for my order. As my eyes scanned the menu I was painfully aware of all the chicken and beef. Jordan's disapproving voice resounded clearly in my head, telling me what an unethical person I was for eating at a place like the Bonanza Burger. My eyes moseyed over to the salad section.

"Do you need more time?" the cowgirl asked impatiently.

"No . . . I'm ready." The salads didn't look half bad, but something was churning deep within me—something that refused to let Jordan influence any of my decisions. Out of spite, I quickly located the most carnivore-friendly item on the menu. "I'll have the Rodeo Bacon Double Cheeseburger Platter and a chocolate milk shake," I said proudly.

Leslie's green eyes bugged out of her head. "Mooooo! Someone's got a big appetite," she said.

"I had a light lunch." I took a napkin out of the dispenser and folded it like a paper airplane.

"So what did you and Jordan talk about after I left?" Leslie twirled a dark curl around her finger.

I tried to shoot the plane at her, but it crashed limply on the tabletop, dive-bombing into a puddle of ice water. "By the way, thanks for abandoning me."

Leslie took a sip of water. "That's what best buds are for. Come on—what did he say?"

"First he told me horror stories about the meat-packing industry," I said.

"That explains the Rodeo Platter."

"Then he told me I was too uptight and didn't know how to lead the band." My stomach did a somersault just thinking about it. "Can you believe the nerve of that guy?" I took a sip of water to calm myself down.

Leslie rested her elbows on the table. "He was flirting with you," she said wryly.

I nearly choked on an ice cube. "Get real, Les."

"I'm not kidding. Didn't you see the way he was looking at you? I'd give my eyeteeth to have a guy look at me that way."

I stared at her in disbelief. *"Jordan?"*

"Don't deny it—you *are* attracted to him," she said.

"Well, yeah . . ." The words slipped out. Leslie had a way of pulling things out of me before I even realized it. "Jordan may be cute, but he's a jerk."

"I think he's really nice," Leslie said.

"So does everyone else," I said scornfully. "Believe me, though, it's all an act. I can see right through him."

Leslie shook her head. "Whatever you say. But I still think he has the hots for you."

What was she talking about? Leslie wasn't the kind of person to make stuff up, but I didn't remember seeing anything unusual about the way Jordan had looked at me. "Even if Jordan seemed attracted to me at first, there's no way he could still like me after the argument we had today," I said.

Our food arrived, and I took it as the perfect opportunity to change the subject. "So who's lucky bachelor number one?" I said, slathering ketchup on my Rodeo Burger.

"He calls himself Spike," Leslie said excitedly. "He's average height, wavy brown hair, blue eyes, likes motorcycles and weight lifting."

"Oooh . . . gorgeous *and* dangerous. There must be a mistake, because that doesn't describe anyone at our school," I said dryly.

Leslie pursed her lips. "Thanks for the vote of confidence." She looked up, squinting slightly, then her eyes grew wide. "Gary's headed this way! I think he's showing Spike to his booth!"

Gary stopped right in front of the designated booth and stepped aside. Bachelor number one took his seat.

Leslie's cheeks turned bright red.

Looking out of the corner of my eye, I started to laugh. Spike turned out to be Vince Tannen, a guy we'd known since the first grade. He was nice, but as far from gorgeous and dangerous as anyone could be.

26

Sure, he had blue eyes, but his wavy brown hair was more on the frizzy side. Vince really did love motorcycles, though. He had a collection of miniature plastic models that he put together as a hobby. And as far as weight lifting went, I could only guess from the look of his skinny frame that he'd probably made that one up.

"Don't say anything," Leslie scolded me as I opened my mouth to make some comment. "This is why I made five dates."

Leslie never approached the booth to let Vince know that she was Sabrina. She didn't even look in his direction to say hi. After a while, when no one showed up, Vince left. He didn't look particularly upset—he probably realized how silly it was to get a date through E-mail. Still, I couldn't help feeling sorry for him. Leslie's plan was carrying things just a little too far.

Bachelor number two, aka Valentino, loved walking barefoot on the beach and watching the sun rise over the ocean. He called himself a hopeless romantic, and although it could've been true, when Leslie saw Valentino's huge nose and gangly body, she decided not to bother finding out.

I had long finished my Rodeo Platter when Leslie snubbed potential dates numbers three and four. Rocker had an annoying habit of picking his teeth with a soda straw, and a very hairy Teddy Bear made the most of his time by doing his physics homework while he waited.

The sun was sinking behind the row of pine trees across the street. "What a bunch of losers!" Leslie said with a yawn.

"Maybe they're not so bad." I drained the last bit of my chocolate milk shake. "You liked the letters they wrote you, so maybe you should give one of them a chance."

Leslie shook her head. "You don't understand how it is, Rebecca. When you write to someone over the computer, you get a certain picture in your head of what they look like. If the real person doesn't match your expectations, it just doesn't work."

"Then maybe you shouldn't meet them at all," I said, shrugging.

"That's a defeatist attitude," Leslie said with conviction. "There's got to be someone out there for me. I still have one more to go—Dr. Gorgeous. I can't give up yet."

Suddenly there was a great deal of noise and commotion coming from the front of the restaurant. I turned my head to see what was going on. A bunch of girls had walked through the door, and they were crowded around in a tight group, all talking and pointing at once.

"It looks like our exchange student has finally made it," Leslie said. "And he isn't a disappointment after all. I'm surprised my hunk radar didn't go off."

I craned my neck to get a better view. It was hard to see with the pack of girls swarming around him. Gary showed the group to the big circular booth in the corner of the restaurant, and as they took their seats I was finally able to get a good look at him.

And then I knew why no one had gone to lunch.

Antonio Ramirez was the most beautiful guy I had ever seen. There was no other way to describe him. He was tall and lean, impeccably dressed in a black sport coat and tailored pants, with a powder blue T-shirt underneath. His silky black hair was chin-length, and every time he turned his head, a wisp of hair fell across his dark, perfectly chiseled face. Antonio had a serious, brooding way about him, but every once in a while his lips would part into a magnificent, blinding smile.

"He's unreal," I said weakly. "He's *so* perfect, he wouldn't even register on your radar. He's way off the scale."

Leslie nodded. "The female population of Westfield High just struck gold, but I wish I could say the same for him," she said, shaking her head. "Look who's making a play for him already."

Valerie Kelmer, president of the drama club, was practically sitting in Antonio's lap, talking his ear off. Her lips were moving faster than a TV car salesman's during a Presidents' Day sale.

"Poor guy," I said. "Do you think he can understand a word of what she's saying?"

Leslie chomped on a cold french fry. "His dad is supposed to be a dignitary or something," she said. "I heard he's fluent in English and a couple of other languages."

I sighed dreamily as I watched Antonio smooth his hair away from his dark, smoldering eyes.

Just then Leslie interrupted my reverie by giving my shin a swift kick.

"Ow!" I shouted. "What'd you do that for?"

Leslie flashed me a look of warning, and I instantly understood. Dr. Gorgeous had arrived.

I tore my eyes away from Antonio. Dr. Gorgeous turned out to be Michael Barber, a senior on the varsity lacrosse team. Leslie's eyes were gleaming, and I knew she was psyched.

"I guess someone else struck gold," I said under my breath. "When are you going to claim your prize?"

"Give me a second or two," Leslie said, taking a deep breath. "It's in poor taste to look greedy." She smoothed down her dark curls. "In the meantime, why don't you go up to Mr. Spain and ask him to the homecoming dance?"

"You must be kidding," I scoffed. "In front of everybody?"

"Why not?" Leslie answered. "You've got enough brains and beauty to run circles around those girls. And it's never too early to plan for a semiformal."

Leslie slipped out of our booth. I heard her introduce herself to Michael. "Are you Dr. Gorgeous? I'm Sabrina. . . ."

I twirled my straw around in my empty milk shake glass, thinking about what Leslie had said. It would be beyond cool to go to homecoming with Antonio—he was so incredible that he'd definitely make up for the previous year's dud date with Arnie. I wouldn't care if I never went to another semiformal again—once you hit the top, it's time to retire.

What are you thinking? said a little voice inside my head. *You don't even know the guy!*

"How bad can he be?" I whispered to myself. Valerie and everyone else seemed to be having a good time talking to him. They probably all wanted to go to homecoming with him just as much as I did.

If you really want to go with him, you'd better act quickly, a different voice said. *You have to go for it.* Impulsively I grabbed my backpack. My heart started beating in double time. "You can do it," I muttered to myself. "You could run circles around those girls."

As I neared the booth my breath started coming in short rasps. *A few more steps,* I thought, looking down at my feet. *Just introduce yourself. Make sure he knows who you are.* I lifted my eyes and caught a glimpse of Valerie throwing her head back in laughter, her pasty white arms encircling Antonio's neck.

Confidence drained out of me like air out of a leaky balloon. Instead of stopping at the booth, I kept walking right past it. *This isn't a good time,* I said to myself as I headed out the front door. *I'll talk to him tomorrow.*

Three

"REBECCA, HONEY, THERE'S a phone call for you," my mom said early the next morning. "I think it's Leslie."

I quickly towel-dried the ends of my hair and went into the kitchen. "Hello?"

"Hi, Rebecca." It was Leslie all right, but she sounded as if she were talking through a hose. "I'm not going to school—can you get my assignments for me?"

"Sure," I said, pouring myself a glass of orange juice. "You don't sound so great."

Leslie sneezed. "Dr. Gorgeous and I took a walk on the Bauer campus last night and got caught in the rain. I woke up with a cold."

I nibbled on a piece of cinnamon toast my mother had left on the counter. "Sounds positively romantic."

"It wasn't so great," Leslie said. "He took the *Dr.* part of his screen name a little too seriously, if you know what I mean."

"I hope you didn't let him get away with it."

"No way. You don't have to worry about me." Leslie sneezed again.

"I still say you should give Donny a try," I said.

"No, thanks," Leslie answered. Through the receiver, I heard the muffled sounds of her blowing her nose. "Call me when you get home, okay?"

"Okay. Take care of yourself," I said, and hung up.

School was pretty dull without Leslie, but her absence gave me a chance to get caught up on some homework before homeroom. When fourth period rolled around, I headed to the computer lab early so I could check my E-mail before class started.

"I can't believe this," I said aloud as I stared at the screen. I typed my password in a second time, but the same message appeared again: *No Mail*.

I knew no one would write back, I thought, feeling slightly sorry for myself. It had to be the line about the date for homecoming—I'd known it would scare guys off. I made a mental note to have Leslie change it when she came back the next day.

"Open your books to page twenty-four," Mr. Meyers said after the bell rang. "For the first fifteen minutes of class, I want you to do exercise number one at the top of the page, and then we'll discuss it."

I opened my book with a heavy sense of dread as I looked at the empty seat beside me. Everyone else in the class was paired up, but I had to attempt the exercise alone. Between the two of us, it was Leslie who had the brain for technology; I did my best to just follow along.

"Before you start, I want to introduce the newest member of the class, in case you haven't had a chance to meet him yet," Mr. Meyers said. "His name is

Antonio Ramirez, and he's visiting from Spain."

I whipped my head around so fast, I heard my neck crack. *Why didn't I see him come in?*

Antonio was leaning against the back wall, waving and smiling at everyone. I sat up a little and smiled in his direction.

"Come up front," Mr. Meyers said to Antonio. "There's an empty seat over here, next to Rebecca."

My heart thumped loudly in my chest. *He's coming over here,* I thought spastically. Chickening out at the Bonanza Burger hadn't been such a bad move after all. *My patience is going to be rewarded. Don't blow it now.*

I inconspicuously tugged at my oversized white cable-knit sweater. I crossed my legs, but I still felt frumpy. My eyes were glued to the computer screen as Antonio slipped into the seat next to mine.

"You're Rebecca?" he whispered to me. His voice was husky and deep, and the way he rolled the *r* when he said my name made me shiver.

"Yeah," I said with a little too much enthusiasm. I looked at him briefly, only long enough to catch a quick glimpse of his incredibly dark eyes. It was too intense, so I looked back at my book. The image of his face seared my memory like a branding iron.

Antonio pointed to the words on the screen. "What is this?"

My face was flushed as I looked at the *No Mail* at the top of the screen. "E-mail," I said, clearing my throat, "but I didn't get any today."

"Could you show me how to do this?" he said. "I would love to know how."

I looked up at Mr. Meyers, who was poring over his

teacher's edition. *What's more important,* I thought, glancing down at my book, *a stupid computer exercise, or getting the homecoming date of the century?*

"Sure," I whispered. I edged my chair closer to his. Even though I still couldn't look at him, I was painfully aware of how close he was to me. His foot, ankle, leg, and knee were perfectly parallel with my own; only a few inches separated us. There was a chance that with even the slightest movement his leg would brush against mine. My pulse was racing out of control.

"I, uh . . . don't know that much yet about how to use it," I said awkwardly. "But I know you need to come up with your own screen name and password and give them to Mr. Meyers."

Antonio pulled a pen and small notepad out of the pocket of his sport coat and jotted down a few notes. His gold watch gleamed under the bright lights. "What's next, Rebecca?"

Another shiver ran up my spine. I turned slightly, my eyes going from his chin up the contour of his jaw and finally resting on his eyes. He was looking right at me.

"What's next?" he said again.

"Oh . . ." I shook my head to snap out of the daze I was in. *What's next?* My mind was blank. I had no idea what was next. E-mail was supposed to be so simple, yet somehow I couldn't recall how to do it at all. It was as if all the circuits in my brain had melted. "There's a sheet somewhere that tells you how to do it," I said, fumbling around in my notebook.

Antonio leaned toward me to look at my notebook. Suddenly I felt the whisper-light touch of his knee brushing against mine. It sent an electric shock through me.

"What are you doing, Rebecca?" Mr. Meyers said, hovering over us. Antonio sat straight up. A few people looked up to see what was going on.

My mouth felt as though it were stuffed with cotton. "I'm showing Antonio how to use E-mail."

Someone in the back of the room snickered.

"You're supposed to be doing the exercise on page twenty-four," Mr. Meyers said. "I suggest you stop talking and get working."

I buried my head in my book. Hot embarrassment crept up my neck to my face. Mr. Meyers returned to his desk. "Sorry," I whispered to Antonio.

"That's all right," Antonio said, leaning toward me again. As he looked at my book, I could smell the warm, spicy scent of his cologne. An electric spark jolted me when his elbow touched my forearm. "Now," he whispered, "where do we begin?"

"Hey, Becky, I've been looking all over for you!" a voice called from behind me.

My computer class had just ended, and thoughts of Antonio had been floating through my mind like puffy clouds—until Jordan West came along to ruin my mood. I shoved my English book in my locker and sighed. "What do you want, Jordan?" I said without turning around.

He leaned against the bank of lockers. "I talked to everybody in the band today, to see when they would be ready to have a serious rehearsal, and everybody agreed that this afternoon would be great," he said. "I wanted to check with you to see if you could make it."

I slammed the locker door shut. "You made plans with everybody for a rehearsal without consulting me first?"

Jordan stood there staring at me, his arms folded across his plaid-covered chest. "I had trouble finding you today," he said defensively.

"You can't just set up rehearsals whenever you feel like it," I said.

"Why not?"

"Because that's *my* job." My head suddenly felt as if it were being squeezed in a vise.

Jordan combed his fingers through his thick hair. "I don't understand you," he said calmly. "After the failed attempt at rehearsal we had the other day, I thought I'd help you out by getting everyone to agree on a serious rehearsal."

I looked up at him, then looked away. *Why does he have to be so cute?* "We can't show up at Joe's whenever we feel like it—he has to know in advance."

"It's not a problem," Jordan answered. "I'll call him right away."

"*I'll* call him," I said. "Besides, that's not the point. *I'm* the leader of this band—it's up to me to do the organizing."

Jordan shook his head. "I don't see why only one person has to take care of the details. The band will never go anywhere if you keep running it like a dictatorship."

My headache grew more intense. "You've been in the band for a couple of days—how could you possibly know what works and what doesn't?" I shouted. "You saw the last rehearsal—no one wanted to do anything but play cards. They're really talented but seriously unmotivated. If I didn't pull everything together, nothing would ever get done."

Jordan's soft lips turned down in a slight pout. "Are you still going to be at rehearsal tonight?"

"I wasn't prepared for it. I have a few errands to run," I said impatiently as I slung my backpack over my shoulder. "If there's some time left, I might show up."

There was no way I'd actually miss rehearsal, but I wanted Jordan to think I would. In fact, I wanted the whole band to sweat it out so they'd stop taking me for granted.

After school was out, I ran over to Leslie's to bring her all her homework, and we talked for a while. I told her all about Antonio. She was thrilled, even offering to stay out another day so I could work with him in computer class again.

When it was late enough so that I thought the band would be getting nervous, I left Leslie's and headed for Main Street. My stomach was tense, and a touch of doubt kept tugging at the corners of my brain. *What if tonight's rehearsal bombs too?* If I couldn't get things under control on a second try, it seemed unlikely that I would ever be able to.

When I walked through the door of Joe's back room, I was surprised to see the band completely set up and jamming away. It was noisy and out of control, but at least they were into it.

"You made it!" Donny shouted, banging the splash cymbal in my honor. "How do we sound?"

"Great!" I yelled over the celestial chords Marissa was playing on the keyboards. I opened my sax case and popped a fresh reed in my mouth, careful not to break it.

As soon as my horn was put together, I joined in on the strange mixture of sounds as we all warmed up. Donny was practicing an old-fashioned shuffle on the hi-hat while Marissa continued on with her space music. Andre warmed up with a funky bass line, and Buzz was going to town with a thrash-metal song I had heard on the radio. I layered over the whole mess with a slow, melodic blues scale.

When my ears began throbbing from the noise, I grabbed one of Donny's drumsticks and whaled on a cymbal. It was our unofficial call to order.

"I'm glad to see you guys didn't bring any cards this time," I said jokingly.

"They're in my pocket," Buzz admitted, striking a chord on his guitar.

I turned on my microphone and looked across the room at the sound board, where Jordan was. "Is everything all set?" I shouted to him.

"It's all ready," he said with a smile. "I'm glad to see your errands didn't take too long."

I adjusted the mike stand. "They didn't take nearly as long as I thought they would." I looked up at the dark bank of lights above us. "Can we have a little background light? It's hard to see over here."

Donny pounded on the bass drum a few times. "What are we going to play?"

"Let's start out with something easy," Andre said.

"Marissa, can you give me a tuning note?" I asked. Marissa played the note, and I adjusted my mouthpiece until my sax was at the right pitch.

Suddenly the room was filled with a flashing white light. Jordan had turned on the strobe.

"You call that background light?" I said with exasperation. My worst fear was that Jordan didn't have a clue about how to use the equipment, adding another strike against us.

"No, I call that a strobe light," Jordan snapped. "I'm not used to this equipment yet. It's going to take me a little while." The strobe stopped, and after several attempts the background lights came on.

"Is everybody ready?" I asked. I started snapping my fingers at a nice, moderate tempo. "Let's try some blues in C major to get warmed up," I said.

Donny had just started counting off when suddenly Buzz motioned for us to stop.

"Before we get into playing, I think we need to talk about something first," Buzz said.

I stepped away from the mike. "What is it?"

Buzz motioned to Jordan. "Come up here, man."

Jordan left the sound board, and a cold sensation hit me right in the gut. I had no idea what was going on, but I had a strong feeling that I wouldn't like it.

Buzz brushed his long bangs out of his eyes, and Jordan took a seat on the edge of the stage. "Jordan and the rest of us were talking the other day about the band, and we were thinking that it would be kind of a waste if we did all this practicing for no reason."

"What do you mean, no reason?" I said carefully.

Andre sat down on an amp. "We don't want to play if we don't have any gigs this year. You said last spring that this time around we'd have some real gigs."

"Do you have anything lined up?" Buzz asked.

I was floored. "Guys, this is our first rehearsal—of course I don't have anything lined up yet."

"You might want to talk to Jordan, Rebecca. He has a few ideas," Buzz said.

"And so do I," I added, glaring at Jordan. "Give me a few weeks, and I'm sure we'll have a show or two lined up."

Buzz nodded. "That's good," he said. "Because I think we all kind of decided that if Synergy isn't going anywhere, we want to bail out."

"No offense," Andre added.

The air in my lungs seemed to have been sucked out of me, and I couldn't talk for several seconds. "*No offense?* You guys are saying you want to quit on me if I can't get a gig together, and I'm not supposed to take that personally?"

Buzz scratched his head. "We'll quit only if there aren't any shows to do."

"I thought we were playing for the fun of it," I said, my voice wavering with emotion.

"I have to admit, it would be more fun if we actually had an audience," Donny put in.

My throat was tight. "I'm really sorry to hear this—but I'll do the best I can."

Jordan tapped me on the foot. "I have a few places in mind," he said. "I could take care of everything."

A shudder ran down my spine. *That's exactly what I'm afraid of.*

Four

"GUESS WHAT I did last night," Leslie said as she brushed her hair in front of the mirror in the girls' bathroom. *"Guess."*

"I don't know," I said, stifling a yawn. "You ate a bowl of chicken soup and went to bed early?"

Leslie looked at me strangely. "If it had been that dull, do you think I would've bothered to have you guess?" She pulled her hair back in a barrette. "I was surfing the Internet with my mom's computer. I found this cool chat network where you can talk to people from all over the world. You've got to come over and check it out."

I ran the cold water and splashed some on my face. I had gotten very little sleep the night before, worried that Synergy was on the verge of breaking up. "I would, but all my free time right now has to be spent on getting the band a gig," I said. "Besides, the whole E-mail thing doesn't seem to be working out for me."

Leslie took a pot of kiwi-flavored lip gloss out of her pocket and smeared some on her lips. "You still don't have any mail?"

"Nope—I checked this morning." I dried my face with a paper towel. "Do me a favor and take my ad off the bulletin board when you have a chance."

Leslie offered me some lip gloss. "I'll do better than that—I'll write up a new one for you. I'll make you an ad that sizzles."

"No offense, Les, but meeting strangers via computer just isn't my style. I like to know who I'm talking to," I said, dabbing some of the gloss on my fingertip.

"You *do* know who you're talking to. You go to school with the guys who send you mail here," she argued. "Give it a chance, Rebecca. Be reckless for just once in your life."

I remembered hearing stories on the news about weirdos who used the Internet to lure victims into meeting them, then took their money or harassed them. It was scary stuff. But Leslie had a good point—since we could send messages only to people in school, it was pretty safe. As far as I knew, no one at Westfield High was a psychopath.

"All right," I said, too tired to debate the issue. "I'll give it another try."

"Cool," Leslie said, dropping the lip gloss into her makeup case. "I'll run over to the lab before class and put in the new ad."

"What are you going to write?" I asked.

"I don't know yet," she said coyly. "But trust me—by the end of the day, you'll have tons of letters."

★   ★   ★

Sure enough, Leslie was right. After lunch I slipped into the lab and found three messages waiting for me. Although I hated to admit it, I was actually pretty excited.

Time: Mon 11:04
To: Lavender
From: Sleeper
Subject: Zzzzzz

> *Hi there, Lavender. This computer class is so boring, I think I'm gonna fall asleep. Liked your note on the bulletin board. I've also been thinking about getting a tattoo. How about checking out a few designs with me on Saturday?*
>
> *Talk to you later,*
> *Sleeper*

Tattoos? What had Leslie written on my bulletin board message? I had no interest in going out with Sleeper, whoever he was, but suddenly I felt a little reckless. I moved on to the next message.

Time: Mon 12:00
To: Lavender
From: Dr. Gorgeous
Subject: Want to meet you

> *Meet me near the tennis courts after school. I'll be the one you can't resist.*

This guy really gets around, I thought, chuckling to myself as I deleted the message. I'd learned from Leslie's mistakes. I hoped the third message would be better.

Time: Mon 12:14
To: Lavender
From: Carlos
Subject: Hi!

>*Hi, Lavender!*
>*How are you today? This is my first time trying E-mail. I saw your message posted on the bulletin board, so I thought I'd try it out. This is kind of weird, but it's fun too. Please let me know if you get this message, and if you want to be E-mail pals, that would be great.*
>
>*Have a nice day!*
>*Carlos*

Should I write back to Carlos? I couldn't decide. He seemed pretty nice. And like Leslie had said, there was no risk involved. If I didn't like the guy, all I'd have to do would be to shut the computer off.

"Go for it, Rebecca," I whispered under my breath. So, with sweaty fingertips, I began typing away.

To: Carlos
From: Lavender
Subject: Hi back!

>*Hi, Carlos!*

*Thanks for your message. I hope your
day is going well. You're right about how
weird this E-mail thing is!*

Take care,
Lavender

My message was short and impersonal, but I
didn't know what else to write. What do you say to
someone you don't know, someone you can't even
see or hear?

I thought about rewriting the note, but then the
bell rang, signaling the end of lunch, so I sent the
message off exactly as it was. *It's the best I can do,
Carlos*, I thought silently. *Take it or leave it.*

Instead of starting my precalculus homework
during study hall, I decided to search for a club for
Synergy to play in. I borrowed a phone book from
the librarian and took a copy of the local newspaper
off the reading desk. Flipping through the yellow
pages and scanning advertisements, I made a list of
every venue within a fifty-mile radius of Westfield.

This is going to be a piece of cake, I thought as
the list grew longer. I wrote down the phone numbers next to the names of the places so I could call
when I got home. Finding a gig wouldn't be hard—
it was just going to take a little legwork.

"What are you doing?" Out of nowhere, Jordan
appeared behind me.

I jumped about ten feet. "Could you not sneak
up behind me like that?"

"Sorry," he apologized. Even though I hadn't

invited him to stay, he took a seat next to me. He looked at the list. "Working on the gig?"

I returned to compiling the list. "Yeah," I said flatly.

"If you need any help, my invitation still stands," he offered.

"Thanks," I answered, "but I think I have it covered." Looking at him, I noticed for the first time how perfectly white and straight his teeth were. They were almost *too* perfect. *I bet they're all capped,* I thought.

Jordan reached over in front of me, the sleeve of his blue plaid shirt sweeping across my bare arms. He studied the list. "If we cut this in half, I bet we could book a gig in no time."

I closed my notebook. "Is there a particular reason why we should rush?"

"No reason," he said, the corners of his full lips turning down. "But the guys seemed pretty anxious to have an audience."

"You know what's really funny?" I asked in a sarcastic tone. "Before you joined the band, everybody seemed content with the way things were. Now they're threatening to quit on me. Can you explain that?"

Jordan's thick eyebrows knitted together in a frown. "Are you saying that I gave them the idea?"

"What exactly did you guys talk about the night you went out for pizza?" I asked accusingly.

He shrugged. "I don't really remember . . . we talked about all kinds of stuff."

"I bet you did," I said. Out of the corner of my eye, I spotted a tall figure dressed in black walk through the door and stop at the librarian's desk. It was

Antonio. "Thanks for the chat, but I've got to go," I said, grabbing the phone book and the newspaper.

"We can talk about this later, if you want," Jordan called.

I shook my head. "I don't think I want to." *I'm glad that's over,* I thought as I walked up to the librarian's desk.

I took a deep breath and smiled, trying to switch from confrontation mode to flirtation mode in less than fifteen seconds.

"Hi, Antonio," I said lightly, plopping the phone book on the desk. "How are you?" Already my pulse was starting to race.

He gave me a smoldering smile. "I'm fine, Rebecca. And you?"

"Wonderful!" I gushed. *Tone it down,* a voice scolded me. *Take it easy.* "I'm sorry about computer class the other day. I didn't mean to get you in trouble."

Antonio leaned against the counter and unbuttoned his sport jacket. I could see his chest muscles rippling underneath his tight black T-shirt. "I'm the one who's sorry," he said huskily.

I swallowed hard. "If you want, I could meet with you sometime to show you how to use E-mail."

"Thanks, but someone has already shown me how," he said. "I sent a letter today. It was lots of fun."

My heart sank a little. "It is fun."

Antonio picked up his books and smiled. "Maybe I'll see you in the computer lab sometime."

I nodded. "Maybe you will."

"Are you sure you don't have any openings until July?" I said into the phone receiver.

The guy at the other end sounded as if he was beginning to lose his patience. "I already told you, we do bookings way in advance. Send us a tape, and if we like you, we'll set you up for sometime in the middle of the summer."

"Thanks for your time," I said with annoyance before slamming down the receiver. I picked up my pen and drew a thick red line through the Zodiac Club. It was the last name on the list.

Getting a gig was tons harder than I'd thought. Every place was already booked up several months ahead, plus they wanted a studio-quality demo tape to listen to before they'd even consider letting a band play. We didn't have the money to do a tape—we didn't even have any songs that were polished enough to be recorded.

There has to be someone in town who'll let us play. I racked my brain to come up with an answer, and then suddenly it dawned on me. "Of course," I said aloud. "Why didn't I think of it before?"

I quickly dialed the number. "Joe? This is Rebecca—I have a question to ask you."

"What's up, Rebecca?"

"It has to do with the band," I said. "The guys want to start playing for audiences, but I'm having trouble booking a gig for us. I was wondering if we could do a show at the café."

There was a pause, and I gritted my teeth, waiting for the answer.

"Jordan asked me that the other day," Joe said.

"He did?"

"But unfortunately, I had to say no—we're booked solid until the spring. But I did tell him that if someone cancels on me at the last minute, I'll try to get you guys in," Joe explained. "Jordan didn't tell you about this?"

"No, he didn't," I said sourly.

"I'm surprised," he said. "Anyway, I'm sorry I can't help you more than that, but you can keep using the back room as your practice space."

"Thanks, Joe," I said, and hung up.

Resting my head on the kitchen table, thoughts swirled around in my brain. *What's going to happen if I can't get us a gig? Will the band really quit on me?* Synergy had been so close the year before; we'd been practically inseparable. Something fundamental had changed during the summer . . . or was it Jordan's presence that was making them act that way? Almost instantly he had become good friends with the rest of the band, and I was left on the outside.

Something in my head suddenly clicked, and everything became crystal clear to me. Buzz, Andre, Marissa, and even Donny didn't want the band to break up—and not having an audience wouldn't stop them from playing. It was just a ploy. If I didn't come through with a gig, everyone would pretend to quit. Then they'd start up another band together, this time without me.

And it wasn't too hard to figure out who would be taking my place as manager of the band.

Five

Time: Tue 7:34
To: Lavender
From: Carlos
Subject: Good morning!

Dear Lavender,

How's my E-mail pal doing today? I'm pretty tired. I didn't get much sleep last night—too overwhelmed by the weird things that have been happening to me lately. I hope things are going better for you.

Let me tell you a little bit about myself—without giving too much away! I'm a pretty nice guy who likes meeting new people. I love to travel. School is all right, but I can't wait to be on my own so I can explore the world.

Did I tell you that I love the smell of lavender? Once, when I was traveling with my family through Switzerland, we came upon a huge field of small shrubs with greenish gray leaves and tiny purple blossoms. When the wind changed direction, I remember the sweetest perfume coming off the field. It was incredible.

I'm feeling better already. Have a great day!
Carlos

Time: Tue 7:50
To: Carlos
From: Lavender
Subject: Glad you're feeling better

Hi, Carlos—
Thanks for your note. I like to travel too, but I haven't done much of it. I've been to Canada, all the states on the East Coast, and California, and once I spent a week in Ireland. I would love to go through Europe sometime, maybe when I get to college. I know what you mean about school being a drag. Sometimes I feel like I'm just biding my time until something better comes along. I can't wait to get out and experience the world.

There's not too much I can tell you about myself. I like what you said about not wanting to give anything away. I'd rather not tell you who I am, at least not now.

Talk to you later—
Lavender

"I told you it would work, Lavender!" Leslie shrieked in the cafeteria when I showed her the printout of the message Carlos had sent.

"Shhh!" I hissed, praying no one had heard her. "Don't give me away!"

Leslie toyed with the curly ends of her ponytail. "This guy sounds so romantic. When are you two going out?"

"It's too early for me to start thinking about dating him." I pulled the lid off a container of strawberry yogurt and stirred the yogurt with a spoon. "Besides, he could be a complete phony."

"Or he could be for real," Leslie added.

I didn't have much to go on, but judging from the two letters Carlos had sent me, he seemed sweet, worldly, sensitive, and maybe too good to be true. I wasn't about to let myself get sucked in by his words until I had a bit more information to go on.

I folded the paper up and shoved it in my pocket. "I can't spend my time wondering if Carlos is for real or not. I've got much bigger problems to deal with," I said. "This whole band thing is really getting me down. Do you have any idea how hard it is to get a gig in this . . ." My voice trailed off into oblivion as soon as I caught sight of Antonio entering the cafeteria. My eyes followed him as he swaggered over to the rack of lunch trays.

"Let me guess—the Latin lover has just walked in," Leslie said without looking up from her slice of pizza.

"How did you know? Did your radar go off?"

Leslie shook her head. "No. I just have to listen to you. Your brain turns to total mush every time he comes within ten feet of you."

She was right. The more I saw of Antonio, the harder I fell for him. Everywhere I looked, he was there, flashing his gleaming white teeth or running his fingers through his silky dark hair. Every gesture he made was elegant and sultry. Antonio was like the huge diamond necklace I had once seen in a jewelry store window— unique, blindingly beautiful, and completely out of reach.

"You'd better start working on him," Leslie said, picking all the green peppers off her veggie slice. "The homecoming dance is only a month away."

I swallowed a spoonful of yogurt. "After seeing him in the library yesterday, I realized I don't stand a chance, Les. Especially not with Valerie Kelmer on his trail."

As if on cue, Valerie came bounding from the other side of the cafeteria over to where Antonio stood. She threw her arms dramatically around his neck and made high-pitched squealing noises in an obvious attempt to get everyone's attention. I studied Antonio's reaction, but I couldn't tell if he found her half as annoying as I did.

"She makes me sick." Leslie grimaced. "That girl has no shame."

"Do you think he likes her?"

Leslie's eyes narrowed. "How could he?"

I frowned. "She's pretty."

"Pretty dizzy," Leslie answered. "Why doesn't he tell her to get lost?"

I shrugged. "Maybe he thinks all American girls are like that."

Leslie tossed a slice of mushroom on my plate.

"It's up to you to set him straight," she said. "Do it for the good of your country."

Valerie led Antonio to a circular table near the windows, where the basketball cheerleaders hung out. They all seemed incredibly glad to see him. "The competition's too fierce," I said. "I don't want to be disappointed."

Leslie held on to the sleeve of my gray cardigan. "Am I going to have to remind you about a certain embarrassing homecoming date named Arnie?"

"All right!" I said in a panic. "I'll work on it."

When I went to my locker during seventh-period study hall, I found a mysterious envelope wedged in the door. On the outside *To Rebecca* was written in handwriting I didn't recognize. *Who could it be from?* I wondered as I tore open the envelope.

> *Becky,*
> *Here's a few places in Portland you might want to check out:*
>
> *Tarantula's Spider Diner*
> *Big Daddy V's Rib-O-Rama*
> *The Dungeon Club*
> *Flash Flood City*
> *Gigi's Imperial Tea Emporium*
>
> *If you need any help setting up a gig, you know where to find me.*
>
> *Jordan*

"Very funny, Jordan," I said aloud, my jaw clenched. I crumpled the letter and the envelope and threw them into the nearest trash bin. "You're the last person I'd call if I needed any help."

Seething with anger, I headed down the empty sophomore wing toward the computer lab. Hot blood flushed my cheeks, and my eyes started to sting with tears. *I can't believe how insensitive he is.* Everyone thought Jordan was charming and nice, but I knew it was all a big act. It was just like Jordan to make fun of me when things were getting tough. After all, it was to his advantage to see me fail.

At the other end of the hall, the door to the computer lab opened, and a few students walked out. I caught a glimpse of a guy with a red plaid shirt tied around his waist. It took me only a second to realize it was Jordan.

I can't let him see me, I thought, brushing a tear from my cheek. As much as I wanted to tell him off, I didn't want him to see that his letter had upset me. I didn't want to give him the satisfaction of thinking he was going to win.

Suddenly Jordan stopped to tie the laces of his work boots, and I decided to make a run for it.

I wasn't thinking straight at the time; I just wanted to disappear before Jordan was finished tying his boots. Walking backward, I ran a hand along the wall, feeling for a door, and when I found one, I pushed it open and slunk inside to safety.

I made it, I thought with relief.

As the door closed I turned around to find myself face-to-face with Donny. He was drying his hands with a wad of brown paper towels. I was in the *boys' bathroom*!

"What are you doing in here?" Donny said, his eyes practically bulging out of their sockets.

"Oh, no!" I bent down to look underneath the stall doors. "Please tell me you're the only one in here!"

Donny threw the paper towels in the wastebasket. "Right now I am, but a guy could come in here any second."

"Not anymore," I said, bolting the door. "I'm hiding from someone."

"Who?"

Don't tell Donny, a voice inside me said. "A teacher," I muttered. "I don't have a hall pass."

"You can borrow mine if you want," he suggested. "I'll say I lost it."

"That's sweet, but I'll just wait until he's gone." I looked at my reflection in the mirror above the sink. My whole face was beet red. "Besides, I've always wanted to know what the guys' bathroom looks like."

Donny nodded with approval. "Is it much different from the girls'?"

"Uh . . . kind of," I said, making a face at the messy room littered with paper towels. I pressed my ear against the door. The heavy plodding of Jordan's boots echoed in the hallway, beating in time to my pounding heart.

"Can I leave now, or are you taking me hostage?" Donny asked.

I waited for Jordan's footsteps to recede. "I guess it's okay now." I unbolted the door. "Please promise you won't tell anyone. I feel like an idiot."

"Don't worry," Donny said, giving my shoulder a squeeze. "No one will know."

I pulled open the door, and to my absolute horror, Antonio was standing right there. I gasped and jumped back. My knees sort of gave out, and I fell against Donny, who struggled to keep me on my feet.

"Hello, Rebecca," Antonio said. With one eyebrow arched, he looked at me, then Donny, then at the sign on the door. His full lips twitched in amusement. "Is it all right if I come in?"

Completely mortified, I said nothing. I didn't dare look at him, either. Instead, my eyes focused on the shiny leather of his black boots.

"She's not feeling too well," Donny said as he started pushing me out the door. "The bathroom's all yours now."

As the door closed behind us, I felt my body go slack. "Do you have a hole I can crawl into?" I groaned.

"Don't let it get to you. He probably didn't think anything of it," Donny said.

"Yeah, right," I said, feeling totally humiliated. "Thanks for covering for me, though."

"Anytime, Rebecca," Donny said, heading toward the library. "I'll see you at rehearsal."

There was little chance of my getting any computer homework done now that school was almost over for the day, but I decided to go to the lab anyway to check my E-mail. I took a deep breath to clear my head and felt the heat subsiding from my cheeks. The computer lab was quiet and nearly empty, except for a girl typing away at the corner terminal. Someone else must've stepped out for a moment, because one of the terminals was on and a few books and papers were scattered across the desktop. I sat down in the next row.

Logging on, I was surprised to see that I actually had mail. I'd left a message only a few hours earlier—would Carlos write back so fast? I hit a few keys and watched the letter scroll up the screen.

Time: Tue 14:04
To: Lavender
From: Carlos
Subject: Hello again

> *Dear Lavender,*
> *I was walking by the computer lab and I couldn't resist dropping you a quick note. Do you ever have days when nothing seems to be going right? My whole week has been that way. Everything I touch seems to fall apart. I'm starting to wonder if maybe I'm jinxed. Sorry to complain to you—I generally keep my complaints to myself. On the outside, I don't let on that anything is bugging me, and I think I seem pretty confident and easygoing. It's easier than having to explain things to people who aren't really interested anyway. I don't mind telling you, though, because I have a feeling you understand.*
> *Tonight I'm going to watch the sunset. I go to this small hill, not too far from where I live, that overlooks a cornfield. I go there as often as I can because it's a good place to*

think. I sit and watch the colors spread out from the horizon like rippling water until it gets dark. Have you ever done this? I'm not talking about just looking at a sunset, but really studying it. The most amazing thing is, every single one is different.

Please write if you can. I'd love to hear from you.

> *Take care,*
> *Carlos*

Carlos's letter left me sitting in the computer lab with a big, goofy grin on my face. He seemed like such a sweet guy. *Don't fall for it,* a voice in my head said. *He's a phony.* I had known most of the guys I went to school with since the first grade, and I could guarantee that none of them were sensitive, caring world travelers with any real prospects for the future. Either Carlos was a first-class liar or I was a lousy judge of character.

Someone walked in and sat down at the computer that had been left on. I glanced over my shoulder and saw Antonio looking back at me.

"Are you feeling better?" he asked. "Can I help you with anything?"

This guy must think I'm a total weirdo. A burning sensation crept up my neck. *Any chance I had with him is totally gone.* "I'm okay," I mumbled, turning back to my computer.

"That's good," he answered in his thick accent. "Are you practicing your E-mail?"

"Yeah," I muttered. *Is that all you can say? I*

chastised myself. It was the perfect opportunity to strike up a conversation, and I couldn't make my mouth work. My stomach clenched like a tight fist. I stared blankly at the computer screen, trying to forget that the guy I was totally infatuated with was sitting right behind me. I tried to reread Carlos's letter, but I was too distracted by the smell of Antonio's spicy cologne, which was wafting in my direction, to write anything back.

Then I noticed something interesting.

At the top of Carlos's letter, just above my screen name, was the time the message had been sent. It was 14:04—that's 2:04 in the afternoon to you and me. I looked at my watch. 2:10. Whoever Carlos was, he couldn't be too far away.

The final bell rang, and the girl in the corner got up and left. I looked around at the empty room. Aside from the girl and Antonio, no one else had been in the lab in the last five minutes.

A chill ran down my back. *Is Carlos really Antonio?*

A deliciously warm feeling filled me as I toyed with the idea. Never in a million years had I thought that it might be Antonio. I scanned his letters, looking for possible clues, to see if they checked out.

Clue #1: Carlos said he loved to travel and meet new people—definitely the exchange student type.

Clue #2: Carlos mentioned going to Switzerland, and so obviously he'd been through Europe; that was an easy thing to do if you lived in Spain.

Clue #3: Carlos was very sensitive and romantic—
that didn't prove he was Antonio, but it didn't
disprove it, either.

Clue #4: Carlos was a Spanish name.

The evidence was overwhelming—Carlos and
Antonio had to be the same person.

What should I do? A lightning bolt of panic
struck me. *Should I tell Antonio I'm Lavender?* It
sounded simple enough, but I couldn't face him
after the bathroom incident. Still, it was a perfect
opportunity to reveal my identity. What if I didn't
get another chance?

Then suddenly I had an idea. Antonio and I
were the only two people in the room. If I wrote
him a quick message, then sent it to him immediately, he'd be able to put the clues together himself.
I wouldn't sign my real name, but he'd know it
came from me—I was the only one in the computer lab! It was a brilliant scheme—Leslie couldn't
have done better herself.

Furiously I typed a message, praying the entire
time that he wouldn't leave before I was done. I
wrote something about sunsets, telling him to keep
his chin up. I tried to be as sensitive and under-
standing as I could in less than two minutes.
Without hesitating, I sent the message.

I quickly turned off the computer, not wanting to be around when Antonio put the pieces of
the puzzle together. What would he think when
he figured it all out? Would he be excited or disappointed?

I turned and looked at Antonio, my heart beating a mile a minute. I smiled at him. "Bye," I said quickly as I shoved the chair under the desk.

Antonio smiled and nodded. "Bye, Rebecca. See you tomorrow," he said, then lowered his eyes back to the computer monitor.

I hurried out of the room as fast as I could, feeling like a bomb that was about to explode.

Six

"**W**HAT A GORGEOUS day," I sang softly to myself as I left for school the next morning. A few leaves on the huge maple tree near the end of our driveway were already starting to turn red, contrasting sharply with the crisp blue sky. It was the kind of day that usually made me want to skip school and go apple picking or hiking or horseback riding in the woods. But that day was different. As I reached the end of the driveway, I realized that more than anything else, I wanted to be at school so I could see Antonio.

Leslie had flipped out when I'd told her the news. She thought the new development definitely put me in the running to be Antonio's homecoming date. In order to increase my chances even more, Leslie lent me her favorite black miniskirt and black leather motorcycle jacket.

"It's very European," she'd said. "You'll make Antonio feel at home."

I stepped out into the road, feeling self-conscious as the cool autumn breeze wrapped itself around my legs. I tugged at the hem of the short skirt, trying to imagine Antonio's reaction when he saw me.

Then my thoughts raced way ahead, wondering what our first date would be like. Antonio seemed to love nature so much, and I wanted to show him all the beautiful sights in Maine. *For our first date, we'll hike up Bradbury Mountain. Antonio will reach for my hand as we walk up the winding path to the top of the peak. Colored leaves will fall down around us like confetti. Then, in a quiet clearing, we'll find the perfect spot to have a romantic picnic. At the end of the day, sitting on the edge of the bluff, we'll gaze down at the miles of foliage stretching to the ocean's edge, near the horizon. The sun will set in a spectacular display of color. And at the perfect moment, Antonio will stare at me with his dark eyes and our lips will meet in a passionate kiss. . . .*

I replayed the scenario so many times in my head that by the time I reached school, I was in a total daze. In the junior wing I waded through the dense crowd of students. I shoved my backpack in my locker but decided to keep the leather jacket on. It made me feel wild.

I turned and headed for the girls' room to touch up my makeup. As I walked down the hall, I looked around for Antonio, but I didn't see him anywhere.

What I did see were posters of cute little foxes and rabbits, with the words *Stop the Killing* printed underneath their pictures. Up ahead was a table covered with newsletters and pamphlets. Jordan was standing in front of the table, holding a clipboard.

Oh, no. I hope he didn't see me, I thought as I spun around and headed in the opposite direction.

"Rebecca?"

I cringed as I heard Jordan call my name. *Keep walking,* I demanded silently. *Ignore him.*

"Rebecca, are you deaf?" he called when I didn't turn around.

A few people were looking at me, and I was trapped. If I ignored Jordan, I'd look like a world-class snob.

"What?" I asked impatiently.

Jordan cocked his head to the side, looking at me curiously. "Do you want to sign our petition?"

Reluctantly I walked over to the table. "What kind of petition is it?"

Jordan tapped the end of his pen against the clipboard. "We're protesting the fur industry. Help us put an end to animal cruelty." He held his pen out to me. "All I need is your signature."

It was a good cause, but Jordan's self-righteous smirk made me think twice. His dark eyes laughed at me, telling me I had no choice but to sign. *You owe me one,* they said.

Why should I help you? I thought stubbornly, making no movement toward the pen. Instead, I toyed with the silver buckle on Leslie's leather jacket, glancing at the literature on the desk.

"This is gross!" I shouted, shocked by the graphic pictures of dying animals. My stomach churned with nausea. "You shouldn't be showing that stuff to people," I said angrily.

Jordan folded his arms across his chest. "I know it's disgusting, but it's the reality of the fur industry.

People need to know the truth so they can make informed decisions."

"People can get the general idea without seeing such horrible pictures," I said, my voice growing louder. "Do you get some sick, twisted pleasure out of shocking people?"

Jordan's eyebrows arched in surprise. "You're calling *me* sick and twisted? You're the one who's wearing a dead cow on your back."

Everyone was looking at us. I dropped my hands to my sides, the scent of leather making me feel queasy. It was obvious that Jordan was doing his best to undermine any bit of self-confidence I had—first with the band, and then with what I was wearing. He made me feel like a disgusting freak.

"Instead of worrying so much about animal cruelty, maybe you should start thinking about how you treat *people*," I said, knocking the pen out of his hand. "And I'm not about to stick around and let myself be insulted by a people-hating vegetarian hippie!"

"No mail again?" I said aloud, staring at the screen. Nothing was going right—first I'd had that run-in with Jordan, and then I didn't have any E-mail from Carlos. I'd already checked eight times, and the day was only half over.

Maybe I typed in my password wrong. I typed it in again, slowly this time, just to be sure. There was a five-second pause, then *No Mail* came up again.

"This isn't my day," I said as I logged off. I felt deflated, beaten, crushed. The fact that Carlos hadn't written back to me was a sure sign that my theory was correct—Carlos and Antonio were the same person. Antonio must've read my message, realized I was Lavender, and been incredibly disappointed. He'd probably been hoping for someone more glamorous, such as Valerie Kelmer.

I walked into the cafeteria, my arms hanging heavily at my sides. Nothing seemed important anymore—not the band, not the homecoming dance, nothing. As far as I was concerned, the whole stupid school could be swallowed up by a black hole and it wouldn't have made a difference.

As I was standing in the lunch line, someone came up to me and put a hand on my back.

"You're looking lovely today, Rebecca," a smooth male voice said.

I nearly fell over when I realized it was Antonio. I looked up at him, and he smiled at me, his hand resting between my shoulder blades.

"Thanks," I said with a nervous laugh as I inhaled his scent.

"I like the jacket . . . it's cool," he said, pulling his hand away.

"Thanks," I said again. My skin tingled where he had touched me. "It's my friend's."

Antonio handed me a lunch tray, then took one for himself. "It looks great on you—you should wear it every day."

What is going on here? I wondered as we moved through the lunch line. Had I been wrong in assuming Antonio was disappointed after finding out it was me? It had never crossed my mind that he could actually be interested—psyched, even. But there he was, standing right next to me, telling me how great I looked.

"You look good too." My hand shook as I reached for a bag of pretzels. "I love your watch."

"It was a gift from my father," Antonio said as he put a roast beef sandwich and a bag of chips on his plate. "He bought it for me when he was on a business trip in Switzerland." His chocolate brown eyes sparkled.

The thrill of our secret cyberrelationship bubbled up inside me until I thought I would burst. "I hear the lavender is beautiful there," I said with a wink.

"It is." Antonio moved even closer to me, then curved his arm around my waist to grab a brownie off the dessert table.

When we reached the cash register, I looked down to see that the only thing I'd picked up was a bag of pretzels. I was so entranced by Antonio, food was the last thing on my mind.

"Fifty cents," the cashier said to me.

I handed her a five-dollar bill. "How was the sunset last night?" I asked Antonio.

"What?" he said, digging into his jacket pockets.

"The sunset," I repeated. The cashier handed me my change. As she started ringing up everything on Antonio's tray, his face suddenly fell. "What is it?" I asked.

Antonio threw his hands up in the air. "I'm out of cash," he said, seeming very angry with himself. Then he started mumbling a stream of words in Spanish.

"How much is it?" I asked the cashier.

"Three seventy-five," she answered.

"No, Rebecca," he said, shaking his head. "I can't let you do that. . . ."

I handed the cashier my money. "It's all right. I don't mind."

Antonio's mouth became hard and serious. "Keep your money." He picked up the brownie.

Impulsively my hand gripped his forearm before he could put the brownie back on the shelf. "I'll take care of it, Antonio," I said. "You have to eat. It's really not a problem."

Antonio looked at me for a moment, then at the cashier, who was holding my change in midair, waiting to see what would happen. Antonio put the brownie back on his tray. "You are very kind," he said in a raspy voice. "Thank you very much."

The cashier handed me my change. My whole body felt like butter melting in the hot sun. "You're welcome."

Antonio placed his hand on my shoulder, and I silently hoped he'd never move it. "Do you mind if I get a soda too?" he asked, reaching for a can.

"Go ahead," I said breathlessly as I gave my last handful of change to the cashier.

"You are too kind, Rebecca," Antonio said gratefully. "I'll pay you back for everything."

"Don't worry about it," I said, smiling.

I picked up my tray and turned around, nearly crashing into Jordan.

"Nice to see you're in a better mood," Jordan said. His denim jacket was tied loosely around his hips, and the clipboard was still under his arm. A pen was tucked behind his left ear. "We're taking signatures all day. It's not too late."

My smile collapsed and my eyes sank to the floor. *Please don't humiliate me now—not in front of Antonio.*

70

"What are you taking signatures for?" Antonio asked.

Jordan launched into his phony spiel again. "It's a petition to fight animal cruelty."

Antonio nodded in approval. "It sounds like a good cause, no?"

"That's right." Jordan handed Antonio the pen, then looked at me. "You've made a wise choice, my friend."

Antonio handed the pen to me. "Your turn."

"No, thanks," I said, glaring at Jordan.

Jordan's dark brown eyes narrowed, as though he were trying to look inside my mind. "Why do you want to harm helpless little animals?" He frowned. "What have they ever done to you?"

"He's right," Antonio said. "You should sign, Rebecca."

I gripped the pen so tightly, I thought it would snap in two.

"Four thousand fluffy little bunnies could die this year because of your stubbornness," Jordan said with a smirk.

Steaming fury was building inside my head, but I couldn't release it on Jordan as long as Antonio was standing there watching me.

"Sign it," Antonio coaxed.

I swiped the clipboard out of Jordan's hands and scrawled my name on the list.

Jordan held the clipboard against his heart, as if it were a cherished possession. His eyes were soft, and he looked extremely satisfied with himself. "Thank you both so much."

Antonio picked up his tray. "Good luck getting

more signatures," he said to Jordan. "I'll see you around, Rebecca."

"Bye," I said, waving. As soon as Antonio was gone, I scowled at Jordan. "Are you happy now?"

Jordan nodded, tucking the pen behind his ear again. "Because of you, five hundred chinchillas will live to see their next birthday."

I shot him a haughty look. "I wish I could say the same for you."

Seven

THAT EVENING LESLIE dragged me over to her house to show me how to surf the Internet.

"Welcome to the future, baby!" she shouted excitedly as she switched on her mom's computer. "Trust me, Rebecca, you're going to love this!"

While the computer booted up, I leaned my head against the back of the chair, remembering the letter Carlos had sent me that afternoon. I had spent every free moment of the day checking my electronic mailbox, and it wasn't until just before school ended that I'd finally found a message.

Time: Wed 13:32
To: Lavender
From: Carlos
Re: Sorry

My dear Lavender,

This is going to be very short. I'm sorry I didn't get a chance to write to you earlier today, but I've been really busy. I have a feeling you might be mad at me, because you haven't written. Please don't be mad. I miss hearing from you.

Thanks for your letter yesterday. I kept thinking about you as I watched the sunlight fade beyond the trees. Maybe someday we could watch a sunset together.

Your friend,
Carlos

I was intrigued by the fact that Antonio still called himself Carlos. And why hadn't he mentioned seeing me in the cafeteria earlier in the day? It was fine with me—I didn't want our romantic little cyberflirtation to end.

To: Carlos
From: Lavender
Re: I'm not mad

Dearest Carlos—

I'm so happy you wrote to me. I'm not mad, but I was afraid that you might not want to write to me anymore. I'm glad to see I was wrong.

I thought about you last night too. There's a beautiful place not too far from here where you can see all the way to the ocean. I hope I get a chance to show it to you sometime. I think it would be fun.

I promise to write tomorrow—

Lavender

"Wake up, Rebecca," Leslie said, poking me in the ribs. "The show's about to begin."

I lifted my head lazily, my daydream evaporating. "What exactly is this?" I asked.

Leslie typed in a few commands. "It's called a chat network. You get to talk to people from around the world."

I yawned and stretched my arms over my head. "You mean send them E-mail?"

"This is a zillion times better than E-mail. You can actually talk *live*," Leslie said. A list appeared on the screen. "Here we are."

I sat up straight and peered at the monitor. The list showed various "rooms" where conversations were taking place on different topics.

"Where do you want to go?" Leslie asked.

There were so many topics, I didn't know which to choose. "Anywhere, I guess."

Leslie put us in a room called The Chatterbox. Instantly the screen started scrolling, throwing us into the middle of a conversation that was already going on. It looked a lot like the script of a play.

Marty: He doesn't know what he's talking about.
Evergreen: Hi, Lavender!
J.J.: Do what I do—ignore him.
Crystal: I have a good joke, does anyone want to hear it?

Dooley: Hi, Lavender—nice name.
Mick: Our school is trying to shut us down—does anyone know how I can connect to another server?

"Type something!" Leslie said, jabbing my ribs again.

My jaw fell open as I watched the lines slide up the screen. "It doesn't make much sense. I can't follow what they're saying."

"That's because everyone's talking at once," Leslie said. "Imagine you're in a huge room at a party. You can hear everyone talking at the same time, but you only tune in to the people you're having a personal conversation with," she explained. "Evergreen and Dooley said hi to you, so say hi back."

I typed it in.

Lavender: Hi, Dooley, Evergreen.
Scotty: What's the joke?
Crystal: Hang on a sec. I have to ask my friend again so I don't mess it up.
J.J.: Why bother saying you have a joke if you really don't have one?
Dooley: What do you look like, Lav?

I looked at Leslie. "What do I say?"

"Whatever you want," she said. "Make it up. No one's going to know the difference."

I started typing again.

Lavender: I'm petite, with long dark hair, chocolate brown eyes, and a big smile. What about you?

J.J.: You sound like the girl for me!

Dooley: Buzz off, JJ. I was talking to her first.

Scotty: Crystal, are you back yet?

Dooley: Ignore him, Lav. I'm tall with brown hair and brown eyes. And I'm loaded with muscles and irresistible charm.

J.J.: He's lying. I could bench-press him with my pinky.

Evergreen: You guys are being immature.

"They're fighting over you!" Leslie laughed. "You're a love bandit on the information super-highway!"

A surge of adrenaline rushed through my veins. I pictured Dooley and J.J. as two gorgeous hunks ready to fight to the death to win my hand.

Lavender: Please, guys, don't fight over me.

[J.J.: Lavender—do you want to go somewhere to talk?]

"What do those brackets mean?" I asked Leslie.

"It means that only you can read his message, no one else," she explained. "There are private rooms where you can talk to someone one-on-one."

Suddenly my excitement soured into disgust. It gave me the creeps to think that this guy wanted to be alone in a "room" with me just because he thought I was a sultry brunette—which was a big lie, anyway. He didn't know anything about me. The whole thing felt totally sleazy.

"Are you gonna go?" Leslie asked.

"I don't think so," I said, watching the conversation

continue without me. "This is too bizarre."

"It's fun. Don't take it so seriously."

I moved away from the keyboard. "These guys seem too slick," I said. "Carlos is much more sensitive and can carry on a decent conversation."

Leslie gave me a knowing look. "You're really falling for this guy, aren't you?"

Just talking about him made me feel warm and content. "You know what, Les?" I said with a sheepish smile. "I think I am."

"So, Rebecca, did you book us a gig?" Buzz asked the next day at our band meeting. "Are we going to play anywhere good?"

I watched with dread as everyone waited for my answer. I sipped my water slowly, not knowing how to break the news. "Listen, guys—getting a gig is a lot harder than you might think."

Andre frowned at me. "I told you she wouldn't get one," he said, shaking his head.

Donny and Marissa looked disappointed. Jordan didn't say anything, but I had a feeling that deep down he was probably pleased. Things were going just the way he wanted them to.

"Wait a minute, guys," I said defensively. "If getting a gig is such a big deal to all of you, why am *I* the only one who's doing all the legwork?"

Buzz reached for the last piece of coffee cake. "Jordan offered to give you a hand, but you said you didn't want any help."

Jordan tapped me on the shoulder. "Did you ever get that list I left in your locker?" he asked.

"Yeah—and it was really funny," I said sarcastically. "Where did you come up with a name like *Big Daddy V's Rib-O-Rama*?"

Jordan focused his dark eyes on me. "I didn't make those up, Becky. They're real places," he said.

I folded my arms across my chest. "The joke's gone far enough, *Jordy*. I'm not an idiot, you know. I threw that list out as soon as I read it."

"No, I'm serious—they're real places," he insisted. "My dad is a music professor, so he knows a lot of musicians. I asked him to give me the names of a few underground blues and jazz clubs in Portland. I thought it might help you."

Buzz groaned. "Way to go, Rebecca."

A lump of humiliation formed in my throat. I struggled hard against the hot mist of tears that burned my eyes. "How was I supposed to know they were real?"

"It's okay," Donny said lightly. "We'll find something."

"Let's find something *quick*," Andre said in a flat tone. "I'm sick of playing to the walls."

All of a sudden everyone was talking and complaining at once. Too drained to stand up for myself, I wanted desperately to slide under the table and cover my ears. Synergy was coming apart at the seams, and I felt completely helpless to stop it.

Then Jordan stood up. "Guys, cool it a second," he said. "I have an idea, if you'll just listen."

Everyone quieted down almost instantly. Buzz and Andre stared up at Jordan like two puppies waiting for their master to throw them a bone. Jordan's control over the group was impressive, and it made me hate him even more.

"The other day I was thinking of possible gigs

79

for us, and I came up with an idea. It's not a club, but it could get us some exposure and a built-in audience."

"Where? The bus terminal?" Donny joked.

Jordan looked directly at me. "How would you guys feel about playing at the homecoming dance?"

Buzz's eyes lit up. "That would be a pretty cool gig!"

"The whole school's going to be there," Andre said.

Marissa nodded enthusiastically.

Great idea, Jordan, I thought snidely. *If you can get it.*

Jordan smiled broadly. "I talked to the principal, and she said they're going to hire a professional band. But she also said we're welcome to open for the other band."

"Would we get paid?" Donny asked, dollar signs flashing in his eyes.

Jordan shook his head. "This one's a freebie—but at least it's a start."

Relief washed over me. The pressure was off, and the band would stay together, at least for now. Jordan smiled at me, and I had a sudden urge to throw my arms around his neck and give him a great big kiss on the cheek. He'd saved the day.

Are you crazy? whispered a little voice in the back of my head. *He just made you look like an incompetent idiot.* In finding a gig, he had earned the unwavering respect of everyone in the band, while they all seemed to have lost faith in me.

"This is great, Jordan!" Andre said. He plugged his bass into the amp and started playing with new-found interest. "When's the dance?"

"Three weeks away," Jordan answered. "We'd better get moving."

Donny looked at me excitedly. "Do you think Leslie's going to be there?"

"I don't know," I answered.

The room was charged with energy as everyone began to set up for rehearsal. Jordan came up to me, hands on his hips, face lit with excitement. Beneath the bright sparkle of his dark eyes, I could see the smug look of victory.

"What do you think?" he asked, hovering over me.

I was busy putting my sax together, and I found myself paying more attention to the delicious way he smelled than I wanted to. "Good job," I said dully.

"You don't sound very excited."

I jammed the mouthpiece on the end of my horn. "What do you want me to do, Jordan? Turn cartwheels?"

He moved closer. "I thought you'd be happy, Rebecca."

"Yeah, I love being upstaged," I said in a hoarse whisper. "Congratulations, Jordan—you won."

"Won?" Jordan's brow creased. "Was this a competition?"

"Don't play innocent," I said. He was sly and manipulative, and I was determined to call him on it. "It was a brilliant tactical move on your part."

Jordan shook his head. "You are the most insecure person I've ever met," he said. "No—I take that back. You're the most paranoid."

"Call me whatever you want. The fact remains that you've gained the upper hand," I snapped, poking a finger at his chest to emphasize my point.

Jordan held my finger and moved it out of the way. "Listen to yourself. You're a control freak. Get a grip."

My jaw tensed. "You can't even defend yourself—all you can do is call me names," I seethed. "'Get a grip'—how articulate! Mr. Sensitivity strikes again."

"And Ms. Touchy gets bent out of shape again," Jordan countered.

"As if I don't have a reason to be." I stood up, my face only inches away from his. I glared at him. "Just do me a favor, Jordan—stay out of my way."

"My pleasure," he said, staring back at me. "Consider it done."

"I'm in love."

Leslie and I spent lunch period stretched out on the lawn adjacent to the cafeteria. I was lost in thought, staring at the orange, yellow, and red leaves that dotted the grass like confetti after a New Year's Eve celebration. My intense anger toward Jordan and my growing love for Carlos kept me on a constant roller coaster of emotion. From one minute to the next, I didn't know if I was going to be blissfully happy or totally depressed.

"Did you hear me, Rebecca? I'm in love!" Leslie exclaimed.

I picked up a leaf, tracing its leathery surface with my fingertip. "Of course I heard you."

Leslie tied her hair into a loose ponytail. "Then why don't you say something?"

I sighed. "Because you fall in and out of love as fast as the weather changes."

"But I really mean it this time." Leslie rolled

over onto her side and propped up her head with her elbow. "It's the real thing."

"Yeah?"

Leslie nodded, her green eyes sparkling. "He's amazing."

My eyes bulged. "Don't tell me you hooked up with Mark Pierce!"

"No." Leslie giggled. "His name is Edward."

I thought for a moment. "I don't know anyone named Edward."

"That's because he doesn't go to our school."

Now I was intrigued. "Where did you meet him?"

Leslie's lips curved into a smile. "On the Internet."

"Leslie, you didn't!" I shouted. "I can't believe you."

"Take it easy," she said calmly. "Hear me out first."

Getting dates through an ad on a computer bulletin board seemed outrageous enough, but falling in love with someone she'd never seen or spoken with—it was unthinkable.

"Who is he?" I asked. "Or better yet, who does he *say* he is?"

Leslie stared up at the sky, a look of contentment on her face. "He's a college student. He lives in Manchester, England."

I rolled the leaf stem between my fingers. "That's a good story. I bet he also told you he was a distant relative of the queen."

Leslie scowled at me. "I've chatted with him a few times before, but last night we talked until four in the morning our time."

"What did you talk about?"

Leslie smiled at the sun. "Pretty much everything,"

she said. "It's so amazing, Rebecca. We hit it off right away. He's so warm and accepting and easy to talk to. We've shared so much that I feel as though I've known him for a really long time. I've told him things I've never told anyone else—except you, of course."

It was a bright and clear day, yet a sad shadow passed over Leslie's face. I didn't think she was even aware of it. What was she getting herself into?

I bit my lip. "Les, did you go into one of those 'rooms' alone with him?"

Covering her face with her hands, Leslie exploded in a fit of laughter. "You act like I picked this guy up at a party," she said. "Don't be such a priss."

"I'm not prissy," I said, defending myself. "Remember when I went on-line? Remember how I started making things up about myself? It's so easy to get caught up in it, and there's no way for you to know if he's telling you the truth."

"Everyone makes up stuff," Leslie argued. "But if you talk to the same person long enough, you get past that. You find out who they really are." She looked at me. "I don't know why you're so down on it. You're doing the exact same thing."

I plucked a dry, brown leaf out of the grass and held it delicately in my hand. "It's not the same thing at all," I answered. "At least I know who I'm writing to."

"You think you know who he is, but you can't be sure," she said. "And for all you know, everything he's written to you could be a lie too."

As much as I liked Leslie, I thought she was way off base. I could identify with her compulsive need to spend every free moment at the computer terminal, and I understood how easy it was to lose yourself in the process. Still, my situation was a pretty safe one. I mean, I was only playing with guys we went to school with. Leslie, on the other hand, was baring her soul to a complete stranger who lived across the ocean. It was totally different.

"Carlos doesn't lie to me," I said quietly, running my fingers through the blades of grass. "I *know* he doesn't."

Leslie rested her hand on my shoulder. "Look, I didn't mean to upset you. Just don't be so uptight about my doing this, okay?"

I nodded. "Okay."

"I'll tell you one thing, though," she said. "If Edward went to school with me, I wouldn't sit around typing letters to him. I'd make sure we got together. When are you going to ask Carlos to the homecoming dance?"

"I don't know," I said heavily. "I wish he'd ask *me.*"

"A girl's got to take destiny into her own hands," Leslie said. "You can't wait for him to make the first move."

"I suppose." I toyed thoughtfully with the ends of my hair. "But every time I'm near Antonio, I sort of freeze up. He's so gorgeous and smells so great. When he looks at me with those dark eyes, I can't think straight."

Leslie picked bits of leaf off the sleeves of her

gray wool pullover. "Tons of girls would give anything to go out with him."

"I know," I said grimly. "Especially Valerie."

"Exactly," Leslie said, standing up. "And you know how aggressive she can be."

I frowned. "I bet she's asked him already."

"Maybe not, but she'll probably do it soon." Leslie held out her hand and pulled me to my feet. "You'd better get on it, Rebecca—before it's too late."

Eight

THE NEXT TIME I saw Antonio, I decided to go for it.

It was one of those rare moments when he didn't have a flock of swooning girls swarming around him. He was standing in front of his locker, looking through a book.

I walked bravely down the hall, determined to ask him to the dance. But before I reached his locker, fear gripped me. *What am I going to say to him?* I needed some sort of excuse to start the conversation—I'd crumble if I didn't have an intelligent comment to break the ice with.

I could ask him for the four bucks he owes me. As soon as the thought popped into my head, I dismissed it immediately. It would *not* be cool to bring that up. The last thing I wanted was to look greedy.

Antonio closed the book and put it into his locker. *He's going to walk away,* I thought with panic. *Hurry up!* I looked down at the floor and picked up a crumpled piece of yellow paper. It was better than nothing.

"Antonio!" I called as he started to walk toward the double doors.

He turned around, looked at me for a moment, then smiled. "Rebecca."

My named rolled off his tongue so suavely, I felt my knees go weak. I thrust the crumpled piece of paper under his nose. "I found this on the floor, and I thought you might have dropped it."

Antonio took the paper from me, our fingers touching for a brief second. His touch made me shiver. "I don't think it's mine," he said.

"Oh," I muttered. There was an awkward pause. *What do I do now?*

Antonio gave the piece of paper back to me. "I have to go," he said. "I'll see you later."

"Wait!" I shouted as he turned around. He stopped and looked at me. My heart was pounding in my ears. *Say something,* I told myself. *Why is it so hard to ask him out?* "I want to ask you a question."

"What is it?" he asked.

I cleared my throat. *The dance . . . ask him to the dance.* "Are you going to watch the sunset tonight?"

Antonio peered out the window. The sky was overcast, and heavy gray clouds were on the horizon. I bit my lip, wondering why my mouth never said what I wanted it to.

"It looks like rain," he pointed out.

"Yeah." I laughed nervously. My whole body felt warm. I crumpled the piece of yellow paper in my hand and started walking backward down the hallway, my eyes still glued to him.

"I'll see you later," he said again.

"Okay." I continued walking backward. Suddenly I slammed into a water fountain that protruded from the wall, and I stumbled, dropping my backpack.

Antonio looked over his shoulder at me, then continued up the stairs.

"You are such an idiot, Rebecca," I said to myself as I rubbed my back.

"Starved for attention again?" Leslie teased, appearing by my side.

I moaned. "No, just making a fool of myself again."

Leslie smiled gleefully. "Look what I got!" She hoisted a basket filled with yellow and pink roses under my nose. "Aren't they gorgeous?"

I buried my face in the basket and breathed in the roses' heavy scent. "They're beautiful," I said in awe. "Did you rob a flower shop during lunch?"

Leslie giggled. "No, silly. Look at the card."

Among the mass of flowers was a tiny white envelope skewered on a plastic prong. I opened it and read the small yellow card that was inside.

To my sweet American girl—thank you for such a wonderful date. I can't wait until our next. Love, Edward

"That's awesome," I said, hoping I didn't sound as uneasy as I felt. "But what does he mean by *date*? Have you been commuting across the ocean on the Concorde every night?"

Leslie giggled again, hugging the basket. "He means our *computer* date. Last night we walked along the Thames and gazed at Big Ben in the moonlight." She sighed. "Edward has a terrific imagination."

"You actually *pretend* to go out on a date?"

Leslie nodded happily. "Why don't you and Carlos try it sometime? Maybe he could use a friend's computer to go on-line, and you can come over to my house and use mine. You'll love it."

"I don't know," I said doubtfully. "Wouldn't it be better for us to just meet in person at Java Joe's?"

Leslie held a rose up to her nose. "Sure, no problem—all you have to do is ask him out."

I thought about my collision with the water fountain. "It doesn't look as if that's going to happen anytime soon."

"If you go on an on-line date with him, at least you won't be distracted by his good looks. You'll be able to have a real conversation," she said coaxingly. "And maybe it'll give you enough confidence to finally ask him to homecoming."

I looked at Leslie, my lips curving into a slow smile. "How does Saturday night sound?"

To: Carlos
From: Lavender
Re: Saturday night

> *Dear Carlos,*
> *I have an odd request. A friend of mine is hooked up to the Internet, and she invited me to her house on Saturday night. If you have access to the Internet also, I thought maybe you could go on-line and we could talk.*

I know it's weird to have a conversation this way, but as you've probably figured out, I can get tongue-tied in person. There are so many things I want to say to you, and I'm afraid that right now this is the only way I can talk.

Let me know what you think—
Lavender

Time: Tue 12:40
To: Lavender
From: Carlos
Re: Saturday night

Sweet Lavender,
I talked to a friend of mine who's hooked up to the Internet, and he said I could go on-line at his house on Saturday night. I think it'll be fun. I can't wait to "talk" to you.

Until Saturday night,
Carlos

"We need to come up with a set list for the homecoming dance," I said, opening my notebook. "Any suggestions?"

The band was gathered around one of the café tables at Java Joe's, recovering from a long rehearsal. It had gone better than expected, and everyone's mood was light now that we had a gig coming up.

Even Buzz and Andre were being nice to me again.

"Which band did the school end up hiring?" Andre asked.

I glanced over at Jordan, who'd propped his feet up on the chair next to mine. "Maybe you'd better ask Jordan," I said to Andre. "He seems to know everything."

Jordan didn't even flinch. "The secretary told me it's going to be Dazzling Diamond Dave and the Gem Tones."

"They played last year," Donny said with a grimace.

Buzz pushed a strand of limp hair out of his face, only to have it fall back again. "I hate those cheesy fifties cover bands."

Marissa gave us a thumbs-down sign.

"Usually the opening band plays something to complement the headliner," Andre said. "So what should we play?"

Donny's face lit up. "Maybe we could do a tribute to Elvis. You know, play all his number-one songs."

"I'm up for it," Buzz said.

Andre shook his head. "I say we rebel and do the exact opposite of what they play—thrash, punk, techno."

I held up my hands to get everyone's attention. "We don't have to do anything different from what we normally do. Let's just play our usual stuff. Who cares if it doesn't fit with the Gem Tones?" I looked around to see if anyone was agreeing with me.

Jordan nodded. "As long as you pick danceable tunes, it doesn't matter what you play."

"Exactly." I smirked at Jordan, wondering if he really agreed with me or was just trying to get on my good side. "Besides, we'll be playing when everyone is arriving. We're only the warm-up band."

Buzz tilted back in his chair. "Good. I don't feel like learning anything new."

"We need about ten songs," I said, numbering from one to ten in my notebook. "We'll adjust the solos as we go along."

Donny raised his hand. "I vote for 'St. Louis Boogie.'"

"Does everyone agree?" As soon as everyone nodded, I wrote the song title down in the notebook.

"'After Dark,'" Buzz added.

No one disagreed, so I wrote that one down too. "How about 'Masquerade'?" I suggested. It was my favorite of all the songs we played.

"You might not want to play that one," Jordan said, leaning forward.

I dropped my pen. "Why not?"

Jordan struggled for a minute, his mouth twitching as though he couldn't figure out what to say. "It's a little weak."

My eyes narrowed. "What do you mean?"

"I mean it's not your strongest song."

"Masquerade" was my showpiece. It was the only song in the bunch in which I carried the melody alone and had the only solo. I couldn't help but take Jordan's comment personally.

"What exactly do you mean by *weak*?" I asked.

"Come on, guys," Donny groaned. "Please don't get into it now."

"It's all right," I said to Donny, my eyes still on Jordan. "If Jordan has an opinion, we should give him the opportunity to explain it."

Jordan put his elbows on the table, challenging me. "You want specifics?"

I bared my teeth. "Yes."

He glared at me as if he knew the secrets of the universe and I was the privileged one he was going to tell them to. "On the second chorus, when you try to bend the notes in the middle of the phrase, you end up making a weird honking sound," he said. "Try not to hit the notes too hard until you gain some control."

"Since when did you become such an expert?" I asked bitingly. "Or do you think that being a techie automatically gives you the authority to criticize?"

"Take it easy," Buzz said. "Jordan's only making a suggestion."

My cheeks burned hot. Buzz always took Jordan's side. Everyone did. "It wasn't a suggestion, it was a cheap shot." I stood up and walked over to the stage.

"Don't take it so hard," Jordan said.

"How am I supposed to take it when someone tells me my playing reminds them of a goose?" I barked.

"I didn't say that. . . ."

"Not in so many words." I threw open my saxophone case and handed Jordan my horn. "If you're such an expert, let's hear you play."

Jordan paled. "You, uh . . . don't want to do this," he said hesitantly.

"Of course I do," I said with triumph. "Teach me how to play."

Jordan hesitated for several moments, his dark eyes fixed on the saxophone. Finally I had him cornered. He either had to back down and apologize or call my bluff.

He reached out and with a deep sigh took the sax from me. I smiled. One squeak from him was all I needed to prove my point.

Jordan slipped the neck strap over his head and spent a few seconds trying to figure out how to hook the saxophone onto it. He fiddled with the keys, adjusted the mouthpiece, wasted time. Buzz was squirming in his chair.

At last Jordan put the horn up to his mouth and blew. First there was only a hissing sound as the air made its way through the instrument. I watched his lips tighten around the mouthpiece, applying pressure to the reed. The air instantly turned into a mellow, sonorous note. Cautiously he touched the keys, his fingers weaving a gentle but tentative melody. There was no squeaking and no acrobatics. Jordan's music was simple, honest, beautiful.

Was there anything he wasn't good at?

When he was finished playing, Jordan took a deep bow, and everyone, except me, cheered.

"Bravo!" Buzz shouted.

Jordan put my sax away and handed me the case. His expression was serious, but I knew that underneath it all he was gloating.

Donny looked at me. "I just remembered something," he said, changing the mood. "Joe said we can rehearse Saturday night if we want."

"It's okay by me," Andre said.

Buzz raised his hand. "Marissa and I will be there."

We needed the extra practice, but there was no way I was about to give up my computer date with Carlos. "I can't make it, guys," I said firmly. My eyes locked with Jordan's. "I have a date."

Jordan looked at me with curious brown eyes. "Who's the guy?"

I swallowed hard. *I can't tell them anything, especially not Jordan,* I suddenly realized. *They'll think I'm a freak.*

"I don't know," I answered weakly.

Jordan's eyebrows arched skeptically. "You don't know?"

"It's a . . . blind date," I said. "A friend of mine fixed me up."

"Oh, one of those," Andre said sympathetically. "That usually means bad news."

"I'm not worried," I said with self-assurance. "In fact, he's supposed to be gorgeous."

Buzz snickered. "It's a bad sign when they say something like that. He'll probably turn out to be like Frankenstein's monster or something."

"So where are you two going?" Jordan asked.

"Why do you want to know?" I demanded. I jumped up onto the stage and started putting some of the equipment away.

"It's important," Jordan said, following me. He took a seat on the edge of the stage. "If this guy really does turn out to be Frankenstein's monster and you don't show up at school for a few days, we need to know where to look for you."

Everyone was laughing.

I had an uncontrollable urge to pick up one of the monitors and drop it right on Jordan's head. But I controlled myself. I didn't want to damage the equipment. "He's *not* Frankenstein's monster, and I'm *not* telling you where we're going!" I shouted. "Can't we rehearse on another night?"

"I'm going to have to side with Becky on this one," Jordan said. "I just remembered I'm supposed to go out with some friends."

"That settles it, I guess," Buzz said. "I'll ask Joe if we can do it on Monday."

Thank goodness, I thought with relief. *Nothing's going to wreck our date, Carlos. Nothing.*

"Great." Jordan leaned back and tugged at the cuff of my khakis. "Maybe we'll bump into you and the monster somewhere on Saturday."

I pulled my leg back. "Don't bet on it."

Nine

"YOU SEEM TO be in a good mood this morning," my mother said as she handed me a plate of waffles.

"I am," I answered, reaching for the maple syrup. The familiar, comforting smells of Saturday morning surrounded the kitchen table. I breathed in the aroma of freshly brewed coffee, the smoky scent of frying bacon, and the damp smell of my father's morning newspaper.

Dad lowered the front page and smiled at me. "Any special plans for today?"

"I'm sleeping over at Leslie's tonight, so I thought I'd just hang around this afternoon and rest," I said.

My mother nibbled on a strip of bacon. "What are you girls doing tonight?"

I ate a bite of waffle. "I don't know . . . probably the usual. Leslie's parents have a new computer, and she's going to let me play around with it."

My father folded the newspaper into perfect quarters and laid it beside his coffee cup. "If for any reason you change your mind and decide to go out—"

"I'll be sure to call," I finished for him.

As much as my parents loved Leslie, they didn't trust her that much. Her parents were much more lenient than mine were. I was certain that whenever I spent the night at her place, my parents had visions of us going to some unchaperoned party and staying out way past midnight.

"We're going to the Bauer football game this afternoon," my mom said cheerfully. "It should be a lot of fun. Do you want to go with us?"

"Sure," I said, taking another bite of waffle. "I'll go."

Mom jumped out of her seat and opened the fridge. "I'll pack a picnic lunch."

Before lunch we all walked over to the college, carrying the picnic basket, a thermos, and a blanket. Just before the game started, Mom and I staked out a place on the grassy lawn, away from the massive crowd, while Dad visited with a few of his students on the sidelines. The warm sun beat down on us, its heat diminished by frequent gusts of autumn wind. The Polar Bears were cheered on by hundreds of ecstatic fans waving silver and blue flags. Two guys danced in front of the bleachers, leading the cheers, their faces painted in the school colors.

The opposing side, the Franklin Hawks, was a longtime rival of Bauer. Their colors were black and red. Since Franklin was only about an hour away, there was a large turnout for their side too.

"Here we go, Bauer, here we go!" the crowd

chanted in unison. The Hawks started their own cheer but were drowned out by the announcement that the game was about to begin. Everyone screamed, then we stood for "The Star-Spangled Banner," played by the Bauer marching band.

After kickoff, Mom and I stretched out on the plaid blanket, munching on a picnic of sourdough bread, cheddar cheese, apples, and chocolate chip cookies. I gazed at the fiery orange and red trees that framed the football field, and dreamed of my date with Carlos later that night.

Then, during halftime, I heard someone call my name. "Rebecca?"

I shielded my eyes from the bright sunlight and stared up at the figure standing over me. "Jordan? What are you doing here?" I asked.

"I came to watch the game with my dad." Jordan smiled. Instead of his usual plaid shirt, Jordan was wearing a blue and white striped rugby shirt and a denim jacket.

"I almost didn't recognize you without the plaid," I said with a smirk.

Jordan laughed. "It's wash day." He turned and smiled at my mom. "Nice to see you, Mrs. Lowe."

"Nice to see you too, Jordan," my mom said. "Rebecca, why don't you offer your friend something to eat?"

Impatiently I grabbed the bag of cookies and shoved them in Jordan's face. "Cookie?"

To my disappointment, he took two and sat down on the blanket. "Thank you, Rebecca. You're very kind."

"Don't mention it," I growled.

Even though my mom and Jordan had met only once or twice at one of the college faculty dinners, they were carrying on as though they were old friends.

"How's your dad?" my mom asked.

"Fine—he loves going to football games," Jordan said in between bites of cookie. "The funny thing is, most people go to watch the game, but he goes to listen to the marching band!"

My mother giggled like a schoolgirl. Just as he did with everyone else, Jordan had charmed her too. "I have to admit the game doesn't interest me that much, but the band is pretty good," she said.

"I'll tell my dad. He's really proud of them," Jordan answered.

Mom cut another slice of cheese. "So why do you come to the games?"

Jordan shrugged. "Just something to do, I guess. It's nice to be outside and watch all the festivities." He waved a cookie in the air. "Mrs. Lowe, did you make these? They're incredible!"

Another giggle escaped Mom's throat. "You like them? It's my aunt's old recipe."

Jordan took another bite, closing his eyes in ecstasy. "I'd love to get a copy of it, if you don't mind."

"I wouldn't mind at all. Do you bake?"

"Sometimes, when the mood hits me. I love baking bread," Jordan answered. "But I don't think I could make cookies as good as these."

Mom reached over and patted Jordan on the shoulder. "You're sweet, but if you can bake something as difficult as bread, I'm sure you'll have no trouble with the cookies."

At this point I was ready to throw up. I didn't

know what they needed me for—Jordan and my mom had formed their own little mutual admiration society. Bored out of my skull, I braided my hair and watched the game. The Polar Bears were up by seven.

My mother handed Jordan a thick piece of sourdough bread. Whenever she liked one of my friends, she had this tremendous desire to feed them. "Try this," she said. "Have you ever made sourdough?"

"Usually in the summer, when I have more time," Jordan answered as he bit into the bread.

I cleared my throat. "Is there a particular reason you came to visit us, Jordan?"

"I just wanted to say hi," he answered.

I nodded ruefully. "And to eat all our food too?"

"Your mom is a very gracious hostess," he said.

Mom smiled at him.

"You, on the other hand, could use a little polish." Jordan winked at me.

"Always the critic," I said wryly. "It's a good thing you know so much. It makes it a lot easier for you to tell others what to do."

The sun hid behind the clouds, and a cool gust of wind came up. I put on my sweater to ward off the chill.

Jordan nudged my knee with his. "So, are you ready for your big date with Frankenstein's monster tonight?"

A jolt of panic shook me. I'd forgotten that I'd told him about my date. *Nice going, Jordan.* Out of the corner of my eye, I watched my mom's pleasant expression dissolve into a look of suspicion. I wanted to grab Jordan by the neck and throttle him.

"Who's Frankenstein's monster?" Mom asked with a questioning gaze.

"It's a nickname for Leslie," I said with a fake laugh. "Everyone at school calls her that." I glared meaningfully at Jordan, praying he wouldn't contradict me.

He didn't say anything, but he looked very amused. The corners of his lips twitched, as though he was about to spill my secret at any moment.

"Frankenstein's monster?" Mom said, looking confused. "That's odd."

"It's a long story," I said. Gritting my teeth, I turned to Jordan. "To answer your question, yes, I'm looking forward to my evening at Leslie's."

Jordan winked at me. "So what do you and *Leslie* plan to do?"

"We haven't decided yet," I said abruptly.

"Didn't you tell me at breakfast that Leslie was going to show you her family's new computer?" my mom said.

I stared down at the ants on the blanket, wishing I could shrink down to their size. "Yeah, she has a new computer."

"Computer? Sounds like a wild night," Jordan said ironically. "So I guess this means I won't be seeing you around town."

"I guess not," I answered, feeling like the biggest dork in the whole world.

Jordan got to his feet. "I think I spot my dad," he said. "Nice talking to you, Mrs. Lowe, and thanks for the food."

"My pleasure," Mom said. "Don't forget to say hi to your father for me."

Jordan smiled. "I won't," he said. "Becky, have fun tonight with your *exciting* plans."

I sneered at him. "With no chance of running into you, it should be a wonderful evening."

Jordan waved good-bye, and Mom and I watched as he walked across the lawn to the sidelines. "He's a nice boy," Mom said.

"Yeah," I answered sarcastically. "Real nice."

"I'm so glad Edward's too busy to go on-line tonight," Leslie said as soon as I arrived at her place. "I need a break from cyberspace."

I sat down on the floor of the family room, ignoring the pounding of my heart. The computer sat waiting for me on the coffee table, but I couldn't look at it. It was only six o'clock.

"Another late night?" I asked.

Leslie, who was decked out in a pair of sweats, stretched and yawned. "Let's just say that I got up about four hours ago." She sifted through a stack of take-out menus. "What are you in the mood for? Pizza?"

"Sounds great," I said.

Leslie tossed the pizza menu at me. A sleepy smile inched across her face. "I have some news."

"What?" I demanded.

"Edward wants me to go to England in the spring!"

My jaw dropped. "What for?"

Leslie looked at me oddly. "So we can meet, silly. There's a big formal dance at his school, and he wants me to be his date."

"Can you afford it?"

"He's offered to pay for the plane ticket. Isn't he fabulous?"

I wanted to tell her I thought it was a dumb idea, but I was afraid she'd do it anyway, regardless of what I thought. It was better to keep her confiding in me rather than have her run off without telling anyone. "Spring is a long way away, Les. Maybe he should come here first."

"We've already talked about it," Leslie said calmly. "He has too many papers and exams. Besides, I've always wanted to go to England."

I tried a different approach. "What do your parents think?"

"I haven't told them yet. But they're pretty cool about things. I don't think they'll mind."

I'd always admired how lenient the Weavers were with Leslie, but this time I secretly hoped they'd put their foot down. Edward could turn out to be a homicidal maniac.

"That's good," I said dully.

Leslie frowned. "You don't seem too excited for me."

"No—I am," I said, trying to fake it. "I'm just nervous about tonight."

The smile returned to Leslie's face. "Don't be. You're going to have a great time."

When eight o'clock rolled around, Leslie turned the computer on. My breathing was heavy, and every nerve in my body was on edge. I'd convinced myself that this was the night I would finally ask him to the dance, but as the evening wore on I was losing my nerve. I couldn't bear the thought of him saying no.

"You're all set up," Leslie said. "I'll go away and give you guys some privacy. If you need anything, let me know."

"Thanks, Les," I said.

She winked at me. "Have a good time, and don't stay out past midnight."

And with that, our computer date began.

Carlos: Hi, Lavender!

Lavender: Hi. I'm glad you could make it.

Carlos: Me too.

Lavender: It's weird writing to you, then getting to read your response right away.

Carlos: I know. This is going to take some getting used to, but I've got all night.

Lavender: So do I. My best friend does this a lot, and she told me about this cool thing she does when chatting with someone on-line. They pretend that they're actually going somewhere.

Carlos: You mean like an imaginary date?

Lavender: Sort of. Sounds weird, huh?

Carlos: A little, but it also sounds kind of fun. Do you want to try it?

Lavender: Why not? Where should we go?

Carlos: Are you afraid of heights?

Lavender: No. What did you have in mind?

Carlos: I thought we could go to the top of a rocky bluff near the ocean and dance under the stars.

Lavender: It sounds great! How should I dress— formal or casual?

Carlos: Since I'm wearing a tux, I hope you're in the mood to dress up.

Lavender: It just so happens that I'm wearing a black velvet evening gown with dangling rhinestone earrings.

Carlos: Good, then you won't be underdressed.

Lavender: There's only one problem, though— how am I supposed to climb to the top of a rocky bluff in four-inch heels?

Carlos: Good question. I don't want to ruin my tux, either, because it's a rental. I guess we'll just have to take my helicopter to the top. . . . Okay, it's all set. C'mon, hop in.

I was totally amazed at how easy it was to pretend. The nervousness I'd been feeling was replaced by a warm wave of calm that passed through me. Our imaginations took over, and suddenly I was daring and free. Instead of a boring high-school student typing at a computer, I was embarking on a romantic adventure, taking risks.

Carlos: Look down over the edge of the bluff. Do you see the waves crashing below?

Lavender: The moon's reflection makes the water look silvery. The sky is so clear, I can see thousands of stars.

Carlos: Do you like this spot?

Lavender: It's perfect.

Carlos: Now that we've found the perfect spot and the perfect night, would you like to dance?

Lavender: I'd love to.

Our shared dream was vividly laid out before me. I imagined Antonio as clearly as if he were standing beside me—his black tuxedo matching his glossy dark hair, the glow of the moon shining in his eyes, the tender way he took my hand in his as we danced under the stars.

My body felt light, as though I were floating. As we danced my heart continued to pound as I imagined his arms around me. After a while we sat down on the rocks and talked. We talked about things we'd written to each other, ideas we'd had, things that were important to us—whatever popped into our heads.

Lavender: I have a question for you.

Carlos: What is it?

Lavender: If your life was like a videotape, and you could erase, rewind, or fast-forward through any part of it, what would you do?

Carlos: I'd take that videotape out of the VCR and put it on the shelf, untouched.

Lavender: You wouldn't change anything?

Carlos: Not a thing.

Lavender: There must be something you've done or said in the past that you wish you hadn't done.

Carlos: Yes, but I also think I did the best I could at the time. I firmly believe that people do what they can, and that given the chance, they would end up making the same mistakes all over again.

Lavender: Aren't there things you never did that you wish you had done?

Carlos: I don't believe in regret. You only get one shot, so you'd better get it right the first time.

Lavender: Is it better to take risks?

Carlos: Most of the time.

Lavender: Then I'm about to take a risk.

Carlos: What is it?

Lavender: Will you go to the homecoming dance with me?

My heart just about stopped as I waited for his response. I didn't know where I'd gotten the courage to ask him—it was as if someone else had taken over and was typing for me. I was relieved that the question was finally out in the open, but I was terrified to find out the answer.

Carlos: You want to meet in person?

Lavender: Sure, don't you?

Carlos: Well, yeah. It's just that . . . this is so much fun. There's so much mystery to it.

Lavender: The thing is, I feel closer to you than to almost anyone else I know, but we've never even seen each other. Sometimes I wonder if you're an imaginary friend I've made up in my head.

Carlos: Do you think we'd get along if we met face-to-face?

Lavender: Why wouldn't we? Unless the things you wrote weren't true . . .

Carlos: I've never lied to you about anything. Have you?

Lavender: Never. See, we'd have to get along.

Carlos: I guess you're right. . . . Let's do it, then. We'll go to the homecoming dance together.

Lavender: Great! Maybe we could even get together tomorrow.

Carlos: If it's all right with you, let's not meet until

the dance. It would be more romantic that way.

Lavender: So we shouldn't even talk to each other in school?

Carlos: How can we if we keep our real names secret?

Lavender: I hate to tell you this, but I know who you really are. I figured it out a long time ago.

Carlos: Actually, I think I figured it out too. But let's still pretend we don't know.

Lavender: Can we at least keep writing to each other?

Carlos: Sure.

We continued writing until way past midnight, although I was hardly aware of the time. Leslie dozed on the couch. Every hour or so we took breaks, but as two o'clock approached I could hardly keep my eyes open.

Carlos: My friend is kicking me off the computer. I have to go home.

Lavender: That's all right. I can barely keep my eyes open.

Carlos: I had a great time. Let me know when we can meet again.

Lavender: I will.

Carlos: I'm sending a good-night kiss to you.

Lavender: And I'm sending one back to you. Sweet dreams.

Carlos: I'll be thinking of you.

Lavender: Good night, Carlos.

Carlos: Good night, Lavender.

Ten

"Y OU KNOW, REBECCA, Spain and England
aren't that far from each other," Leslie said
one afternoon between classes. We were hanging
out by her locker. "If I married Edward and you
married Antonio, we could meet in France for va-
cations."

I sighed dreamily, imagining Antonio and me in
a beautiful villa just outside of Madrid. "That
would be incredible."

"We'll meet twice a year—skiing in the French
Alps in the winter, and summers in the south of
France," Leslie said very matter-of-factly, as if she
had seen the future.

I leaned my head against her locker. "France
might get boring after a while," I said. "You could
always come visit us in Spain, Sabrina." We had
started calling each other by our screen names.

Leslie nodded seriously. "And whenever
you're in London, Lavender, our flat is yours."

I made a face. "I don't think I want to go to London."

"Why not?"

"The food's supposed to be really bad. I'm not a big fan of kidney pie," I said.

"Gross." Leslie stuck her tongue out in disgust. "I guess we'll be visiting you, then."

"Did Edward mail you his picture yet?"

Leslie frowned. "No—he had a friend take one, but he hasn't had a chance to develop it yet," she said. "Which reminds me—do you think you could take a few pictures of me to send?"

"Sure," I said. I was totally in favor of Leslie's exchanging pictures with Edward. Chances were that Edward would never live up to Leslie's image of him, and as soon as she realized what a goon he really was, she'd drop him like a sack of potatoes.

Suddenly Leslie jabbed me in the ribs. "Future husband alert."

I looked up to see Antonio walk by, with a couple of his friends in tow. I smiled at him, and he turned to me and smiled back. My spine tingled. He was right. It was fun to hold on to our secret.

"Did you see the way he looked at you?" Leslie whispered after he passed by. "I swear, sparks were flying off your bodies."

"Do you think so?" I hated to see him go. More than anything, I wanted to follow him down the hallway, throw my arms around him, and bury my face in his neck.

Then, as if she'd stolen my thoughts, Valerie

Kelmer came bounding out of nowhere and did exactly what I'd imagined. The smile on my face shriveled into a scowl.

"Oooh—future mistress alert," Leslie said. "That girl doesn't miss a trick."

Antonio walked on, as though he didn't know Valerie was hanging off him like an anchor around his neck.

"Why does he let her do that?" I asked.

"He probably likes the attention."

A raging streak of white-hot jealousy ripped through me. After all the romantic things he'd written to me, how could he flirt with Valerie? I wasn't about to stand for it.

"Watch this," I said to Leslie. I strolled over to where Antonio was and stood right in front of him.

"Hi, Rebecca," Antonio said. He looked uncomfortable.

I folded my arms across my chest. "Did you return your tux?" I asked, referring to our computer date. Even though we'd agreed not to talk to each other until the night of the dance, I couldn't resist.

"What?" Antonio said, staring blankly at me.

"Don't you remember the rocky bluff, our night under the stars?" I reminded him.

Valerie pouted. "What is she talking about?"

Antonio shook Valerie off his shoulders and stared at me. He had the best poker face I'd ever seen. Even though he pretended not to understand me, I knew my point was getting across. "The stars?" he asked.

I reached out and smoothed the lapels of his sport coat. Valerie's mouth gaped in horror. "Don't forget what we talked about," I said in a hushed voice.

"No, I, uh . . . won't forget," he mumbled, shaking his head,

"It's a week and a half away, and I'm counting every minute." I looked up at him. "Are you?"

Antonio's dark eyes were wide. He nodded imperceptibly. "Yes."

"How long did that take?" I said into my microphone so Jordan could hear me in the back of the room.

Jordan looked at his watch. "About three minutes," he shouted back to me.

I sighed and paced back and forth on the stage. "This isn't working, guys," I said to the rest of the band. "At this rate, we'll be done with our entire set in thirty minutes."

Buzz adjusted the reverb on his amp. "Let's learn a few more tunes."

I shook my head. "The dance is five days away—we don't have time," I said. "We'll just have to stretch out the songs by making a few adjustments." I felt my fingers grow cold and shaky, the way they always did when I was nervous. I pressed them against my neck to warm them up. "Take down some notes, everybody."

Jordan left the sound board and joined us onstage, where everyone was hovering around me. I opened my music folder and pulled out a few sheets of paper.

"We're going to have to change the road map for a song or two," I said, scribbling a few chord progressions. "When we do 'Bossa Blues,' we'll run through the chorus twice like we said, but instead of getting into the solos right away, we'll hit the bridge. Then after each solo we'll return to the bridge. Got it?"

Jordan scratched his head. "That's still not much time, Becky. Maybe you should also lengthen the solos."

"I was getting to that," I said impatiently. "Let's double up, from sixteen-bar solos to thirty-two. Can everybody handle that?"

"That's fine, I guess," Buzz said. "What's the order?"

"The usual order. Me first, then Marissa, you, Andre—Donny, do you want a solo?"

Donny nodded excitedly. "That would be awesome."

"What's next?" Andre asked.

I looked at the list of songs, unsure of what to do next.

Jordan leaned over my shoulder. "Why don't you do something with 'Firewalker'?" he suggested. He was so close that I could feel his warm breath on the back of my neck.

A strange tingle slid down my neck to my shoulder. I turned suddenly, and my head nearly collided with Jordan's. "What should we do?" I asked, my skin feeling hot.

"Start it with a vamp," he said, his soft voice filling my ear. "Bec, maybe you could do a free solo over it, and when you're ready, signal the band to start."

I lingered there for a moment, letting the words soak in. When my head cleared, I jumped to my feet. "Did everybody get that?" I nervously fiddled with the keys of my sax. "Let's try it out."

I watched Jordan as he walked back to the sound board. The rest of the band took their places.

"'Bossa Blues' first," I said, snapping my fingers. "A-one, a-two, a-one, two, three, four—"

Donny picked up the tempo I had laid down, and Andre's bass thumped a walking line over the drums. As I listened for Marissa's intro to cue me in, I imagined it was the night of the homecoming dance and we were onstage in front of hundreds of people. I imagined that Antonio was out there in the audience, listening to my music. More than anything, I wanted the band to do well—I wanted to impress him.

Make it good, I told myself as Marissa cued me in. I raised the sax to my mouth and blew a strong, steady stream of air.

The warm, syncopated melody came back at me through the small monitor at the front of the stage. My shoulders relaxed. The notes seemed to come off almost automatically as my fingers launched them into the atmosphere, only to settle back to earth, landing squarely in between the rhythmic gaps of Buzz's guitar line. I took liberties with the melody, drawing some notes out and cutting others short. Everything was coming together beautifully.

But as we rounded out the first chorus, it all fell apart. My monitor suddenly cut out, so I couldn't hear myself playing. Instead of repeating the chorus, Marissa went for the bridge, Andre launched into a solo, and I had absolutely no idea what Buzz was playing. Notes were colliding like a pileup on the freeway.

"Hold it!" I shouted over the noise. But they kept playing. The noisier it got, the louder they played. Snippets of Jimi Hendrix songs popped up here and there as the band spiraled out of control.

I grabbed a drumstick out of Donny's hand and went ballistic on the splash cymbal. It felt good to get some of my aggression out. When I was done, the room was silent, and everyone's jaws were hanging wide open.

"That was cool," Buzz said.

"What's your problem?" Jordan shouted across the room.

I smoothed the hair out of my eyes. "For one, my monitor's not working, and second, no one was paying attention to the road map."

Buzz clawed at the air and made cat noises.

"We were just having a little fun," Andre said. "Lighten up."

I threw my hands in the air. "I thought getting a real gig was a big deal to you guys—it's all you've talked about since school started. Now that you have one booked five days from now, you don't even care."

"Don't worry, Rebecca," Donny said, frowning. "Everything will work out. We can play the song; we just have to remember the map."

Jordan came back to the stage. "Since when is the gig such a big deal to you?" he asked, testing the connections to the monitor. "Is a talent scout from a major record label going to be there to hear you play?"

I shot him a nasty look. "My boyfriend's going to be there," I blurted.

"Frankenstein's monster?" Jordan scoffed.

Donny did a drumroll, then a cymbal crash. "Who?"

I smiled mysteriously. "Someone you all know and love—but you'll have to wait until the dance to find out."

Jordan eyed me with suspicion. "Do you really have a boyfriend?"

"*Yes,*" I said irritably.

"Phew!" Jordan wiped the back of his hand across his forehead. "It looks like the rest of the male population is safe from your clutches for now."

"Let me tell you something," I began, my temper flaring. "He's a lot more considerate, kind, and sensitive than you could ever hope to be!"

"I'm sure he is," Jordan shot back. "He'd have to be a saint to put up with your garbage. Don't worry about Saturday night—we'll all make sure you look good for your boyfriend."

I dug my fingernails deep into the palm of my hand. "Are you saying I can't look good on my own?"

A flippant smirk played at the corners of Jordan's mouth. "Every little bit helps."

The day before the dance I was a total wreck.

When school let out Friday afternoon, I saw Antonio approaching as I walked toward my locker. A kind of magnetic force was pulling me toward him, and I had an irresistible urge to kiss those perfectly shaped lips of his. As he came closer the attraction grew stronger, and I felt myself losing control. Our secret had been going on for so long, I didn't think I could wait another day.

But then Antonio looked at me. Standing only a

few feet away, he gazed deeply into my eyes. His look said it all. *I feel the same way, Rebecca. But don't spoil our romantic evening. Wait until tomorrow.*

All right, my eyes said to him. *I promise to wait.* Antonio continued on as if we were strangers, but the communication between us had been clear. Wouldn't everyone be shocked when they found out we were in love?

Humming John Coltrane's "My Favorite Things" to myself, I tossed a few books into my backpack and spun the combination lock on my locker door. My body felt like a compressed spring that was about to let go. Slinging the backpack over my shoulder, I skipped down the hallway, barely able to contain my excitement.

"What's with the perma-smile?" Leslie asked, winking at me. "Are you trying out for a toothpaste commercial?"

"I suppose I could ask you the same thing," I said. Ever since Edward had sent Leslie the flowers, she'd been walking around with a dopey grin too. "We're pathetic, huh?"

"Pathetic but lucky. You still want me to come over tonight after dinner?"

I nodded furiously. "I need you to keep me from going crazy."

"You've come to the wrong person for that," Leslie said with a laugh.

"Well, at least you can make the time go by more quickly."

"That I can do." Leslie put on a pair of sunglasses and took her keys out of her purse. "I'll see you at seven."

I watched her push through the double doors before I turned around and headed for the exit at the opposite end of the hall. The crowd had thinned out a little, and now the hall was filled mostly with members of the homecoming committee, who were staying to decorate.

I walked up the stairs to the gym to take a peek. My stomach started to flutter in anticipation as I stood in the doorway and watched students hanging streamers from basketball hoops. I hoped the next twenty-four hours would go by like a flash, but I knew they would drag on for an eternity.

Turning around to leave, I saw Antonio outside the gym door, talking on the pay phone in the hallway. He was wearing a pair of black jeans and a dress shirt with sleeves rolled up to the elbows, and his silky black hair was tucked behind his ears.

My legs turned to jelly. I could have watched him forever, standing there looking so suave and beautiful. His soft lips moved as he spoke into the receiver, and instantly I was jealous of the person at the other end of the line. I had been patient and strong, but my resolve was breaking down. Longing burned inside me like smoldering coals.

Without thinking, I walked up to Antonio. I stood right next to him, very close, and breathed in his scent. He stopped talking. I leaned toward him, my lips a fraction of an inch away from his ear. My heart thundered in my chest as I felt the warmth of his neck rising to my face. The soft ends of his hair brushed against my cheek.

Then, very quietly, I whispered, "I'll see you tomorrow night."

And before he could answer, I turned around and walked away.

"I can't believe you," Leslie said, curled up into a ball on my bed. "Even *I* wouldn't have had the guts to do something like that."

My head was like a murky lake, with worries darting around like startled fish. I was terrified for so many reasons, I couldn't keep count anymore. What if Antonio and I didn't get along? What if I said the wrong things? What if I made a jerk of myself?

"Can you zip me up?" I asked, standing in front of the full-length mirror on my closet door. "It was temporary insanity," I said. "He just looked so amazing—he's completely irresistible."

Leslie zipped up the back, and we both stood in front of the mirror, looking at my reflection. I was wearing a simple knit dress with a scoop neckline and long sleeves. It draped perfectly, skimming my waist, then falling into a flared skirt that ended just above the knee. And of course it was lavender.

Leslie looked at my dress and whistled. "You look gorgeous."

I turned, watching the skirt swing as I moved. "You think so?"

"Would I lie?"

"I guess not," I said with a smile. I felt as if I were floating on warm air. "You know, even though Antonio is the most incredible guy I've ever laid eyes on, it's his personality that I really love. His letters are so smart, funny, and warm—I've never met anyone like him." I looked down at my

121

violet pumps. "I'm starting to think the shoes are a bit much."

"Everything's perfect," Leslie said.

I sat down on the edge of my bed. "I wish you were going."

"You don't need me there—you've got your Latin lover," Leslie said. She nudged my elbow with her bare toes. "And to tell you the truth, I don't really care about going to a silly high-school dance—no offense."

"You *used* to care," I said, sliding the pumps off my feet. "There's no reason why you can't go and have some fun. You could dance with Donny—he's always asking about you. He's a great guy. You should give him a chance."

Leslie hugged my favorite purple pillow. "I'm through with high-school *boys,*" she said. "Talking to Edward has made me realize that there's a huge world out there that extends beyond the walls of Westfield High. I'm ready to move on."

I piled my hair on top of my head and studied my reflection. "It's great you want something better, but while you're still stuck in school, you might as well have some fun."

Leslie stared off dreamily, her eyes fixed on the opposite wall. "It wouldn't be any fun without Edward. Besides, I'll have lots of fun when I go to England in the spring."

"But that's only for a week."

Leslie shrugged. "If I like it, maybe I'll stay longer."

An icy fear gripped me. Would Leslie seriously give up her family and friends, not to mention her education, for some guy she hardly knew?

"What did your parents say about it?" I asked.

"I haven't told them yet. I'm going to tell them tonight," Leslie said. "I don't think it'll be a problem, though." Opening her backpack, Leslie pulled out four packs of photos. Her face lit up. "Thanks for taking pictures of me the other day. I got them back, and it's a good thing we took four rolls."

When I looked at the pictures, I knew what she meant. Out of all the shots we took, there were only ten that were any good. Most of the rest were blurred or overexposed, and in some I'd cut off the top of her head. In at least eight shots, Leslie's eyes were closed.

The one I liked the best was when Leslie looked as if she'd been caught slightly off guard—she looked the most natural. "You should send Edward this one," I said.

"I will," she said, "Along with all the others that came out."

"When are you getting a picture of him?"

She gathered up the photos. "Soon. He promised it would be very soon."

Leslie seemed to believe it, but I had my doubts. Edward had been promising her a picture for ages. I had the sneaking suspicion that Mr. England was not who he claimed to be.

"I almost forgot," Leslie said, pulling a small box out of her backpack. "I bought you a present."

"You did?" I said, surprised.

Leslie handed me the box. It was tied with a purple ribbon. "It's to wish Lavender good luck on her first date with Carlos."

I smiled sheepishly as I unwrapped the present.

It was a tiny bottle of lavender perfume. "Lavender thanks you," I said, throwing my arms around her.

"And Sabrina says you're welcome." Leslie smiled.

I unscrewed the top and dabbed the perfume on my wrists. As the warmth of my skin released the heavy floral scent, I convinced myself that there was nothing to be nervous about. Everything was going to be perfect.

Eleven

"WE'VE GOT A problem." Donny sat down in a folding chair next to me backstage. "Marissa's keyboards aren't coming out on the sound system."

At forty-five minutes before show time, that was the last thing I wanted to hear. "I thought we took care of everything at the sound check this afternoon," I said.

Donny nervously tapped his drumsticks together. "We did, but it looks like Dazzling Diamond Dave and the Gem Tones rearranged things during their sound check. Now we can't get it to work."

"Where's Jordan?"

Donny hesitated. "We can't find him."

My blood began to boil. Antonio was going to be watching that night. There was no way I was going to let Jordan mess things up. "Don't worry about it," I said, putting my reed in its plastic case. "I'll find him."

"He can't be too far," Donny said delicately. I sensed he was afraid of another big blowup between us. "By the way, Rebecca, you look great."

I smiled weakly at Donny. It was the first time I'd seen him in a suit and tie, and his hair was tamed with a bit of gel. "Thanks—so do you."

"Do you think Leslie would agree with you?" he asked hopefully.

I sighed. "I'm sorry, Donny. Leslie isn't here. She's not coming tonight." A pang of sympathy tugged at my heart as his face fell. "But if she were, I'm sure she'd think so too."

After checking the mirror to make sure my French twist was still in place, I spent the next twenty minutes scouring the school looking for Jordan. The whole band had agreed to meet backstage an hour before the show. It wasn't like Jordan to be late.

Fear suddenly gripped me—what if he'd gotten into a car accident on the way over? What if he was seriously hurt?

Just as I started heading back to the gym to look around again, the door to the boys' bathroom opened. In the dim light, my heart stopped as I caught sight of the blond hair, lean frame, and impeccably tailored suit.

It was Jordan. I caught my breath, relieved that he was all right.

Then I let him have it.

"Where have you been?" I shouted down the hallway.

Jordan looked at me strangely, as if he didn't recognize me. "Hey, Becky," he said after a moment. "I was getting ready."

Is it me, or does he seem a little nervous? I walked toward him. "I don't know why you're spending so much time combing your hair when no one's going to see you behind the sound board anyway," I said.

Jordan's brow wrinkled, and he smoothed his hand over his hair. He looked really worried. The expression on his face made me instantly regret what I'd said.

I could see that this wasn't the right time for our usual sparring, so I decided to get right to the point. "There's a problem with Marissa's keyboards. They're not coming through."

Jordan groaned. A faint mist of perspiration dotted his forehead. "I thought I took care of everything."

"It's not your fault," I said. "You can blame it on Diamond Dave."

"I'll go fix it right now," he said, heading for the double doors.

"Wait a second!" I blurted. Jordan turned around. "Your tie's a little crooked."

Jordan spastically grabbed at his throat as if he were choking. He tugged the tie from right to left, making it look worse.

"Let me do it," I said, reaching out to help.

Slowly I straightened the tie, my fingertips grazing his collarbone and shoulders as I worked my way to the back of his neck. He lowered his head so I could reach, and I breathed in the rich mixture of aftershave and soap that lingered on his skin. It was intoxicating. As I tightened the knot I could feel his warm breath on the top of my head.

"Thanks a lot, Rebecca," he murmured.

"Don't mention it," I said, pulling away from him suddenly. "You'd better hurry. We don't have much time."

"Thank you all for coming tonight," the emcee's voice blared through the sound system.

Synergy waited in the dark, behind the curtain, as he introduced us. My foot tapped anxiously against the bottom of the microphone stand as I looked around to make sure everyone was ready. Since the mikes were on, we relied on eye contact. Donny was all set. Marissa, who looked pretty in a black silk slip dress and lug boots, gave me a thumbs-up. Andre nodded with fright, rocking back and forth on his heels. I glanced over at Buzz. He was wearing the same clothes he wore every day but with a tuxedo jacket thrown over the whole thing. Standing there with his feet wide apart and his head hanging down like a rock star's, I knew he was ready.

"Please welcome . . . *Synergy!*"

I thought I was ready, but when the curtain finally opened and I looked out at the crowd, my stomach caved in. The gym was ten times bigger than Java Joe's and was already half full. I hadn't expected so many people to show up early. They were milling around the tables, and I figured they were comparing suits and dresses, talking about Westfield's victory at the football game earlier in the day, gossiping about who was coming that night . . . in any case, they were hardly taking any notice of us. I scanned the gym, and as far as I could see, there was no sign of Antonio.

"Psst," Buzz hissed.

I must've blanked out for a second, because everyone in the band was staring at me, waiting for me to count off. Andre backed up a little and tripped over his patch cord. His bass got too close to the amp, and high-pitched feedback squealed through the speakers.

People covered their ears and looked at us as though we were a bunch of idiots.

I stepped up to the microphone. "Sorry about that. Our first song is called 'After Dark.'"

Then I turned around and snapped the rhythm for Donny. I knew it was faster than it should've been, but the adrenaline flow in my body seemed to be taking over.

The rest of the band matched the faster tempo and then surpassed it. Pretty soon we were in double time. My fingers were performing acrobatic feats to keep up, but somehow I was doing it. I looked down at the dance floor in front of the stage; no one was making an attempt to dance. I couldn't blame them, since the song kept speeding up until it bordered on thrash. It wouldn't have shocked me at all if someone had started a mosh pit. *Too bad Leslie isn't here,* I mused. *She would've been the first in line.*

When the song was over, I took a huge breath, my lungs struggling for air as if I'd been held underwater. I strolled away from the mike, wiping sweat from my forehead, and met with the band in a huddle.

"Let's take it easy—at this rate, we're going to run out of songs in fifteen minutes," I whispered. "I'll count the others off a bit slower.

Donny, you bring them up to speed if we need it."

I returned to the mike and smiled at the audience, who still didn't seem to notice we were there. "Thanks for waiting. This one is called 'Crocodile Blues.'"

We made it through the next few songs all right, but everyone in the band was so tense that the music sounded strained. But by the end of the fourth song, when still no one was clapping, we started to loosen up quite a bit. It was as if we all realized at once that no one was listening to us play, so it didn't really matter what we did. That's when we started to have some fun.

Whenever I could, I looked at the entrance to see if Antonio had arrived. I didn't see him, but the stage lights were so bright, it was hard to see beyond the dance floor. Still, I sensed that he was there, maybe hiding out in a corner so I wouldn't feel self-conscious. But I did anyway. Every note I played was for him.

Near the end of the set, we sizzled. We were like a pressure cooker that had exploded, our hot notes raining down on the crowd. People started to take notice and were grooving on the dance floor. It made me forget the struggle I'd gone through to get the band together. It made it all worth it.

"Masquerade" was the last song of the set. I didn't care that Jordan thought it was weak—it was my showpiece. I'd been practicing hard and had saved it for the end of the set, when I could be sure that Antonio would be there to hear it.

"This is our last song," I said into the mike, trying to see beyond the dance floor. "This is going out to a friend of mine who's here tonight . . . you know who you are."

I signaled the band, and they started the introduction with a slow and fluid rhythm. I closed my eyes. *This is for you, Antonio,* I thought as I waited for my entrance. There were so many things I had wanted to tell him, things I had never written on the computer. Things I wanted him to *hear.*

Reaching down deep, as far as I could go, I breathed in and hit the first note on cue. My heart felt big, bursting with love for Antonio, the feelings riding on the air I drew from within. I couldn't stop them—they poured out in a steady stream, shaping each sound that came out of my saxophone. It was the best I had ever played.

The rest of the band could feel it too. As the melody crested and fell and the phrases became louder or diminished, for the first time they followed my lead. Whatever I did, they supported me. It was pure magic.

When we finished, the crowd roared. The dance floor was packed with couples clinging to each other. They wanted us to play another song, but we decided to call it quits for the night. There was no way we could have topped that last number.

As the curtain closed I stared out into the darkness, hoping he'd finally gotten the message.

I'll see you soon, my love.

The wait was killing me. Carlos and I had agreed to meet in front of the stage in the far corner, and as soon as the band was all packed up, I raced over to our spot. I had expected to see Antonio waiting for me with open arms, telling me how wonderfully I'd played, but he wasn't there yet.

Come on, I've waited long enough, I thought impatiently. Sifting through the evening bag my mother had lent me, I found the lavender perfume and dabbed a touch more on my skin. Couples walked by me on their way to the dance floor. I felt like a wallflower, awkwardly waiting for someone to notice me.

Then Valerie came up to me. She reeked of cheap Hollywood glamour in a gold lamé dress. Her hair defied gravity, and her mouth was painted an obnoxious red.

So tacky, I thought.

"Rebecca, *enchantée,*" she said, offering me her limp hand. "You were fabulous tonight, darling."

"Thanks," I said with a fake smile.

Valerie's plastic lips pulled into a tight pucker. "It's unfortunate that you don't have an escort this evening."

I smiled graciously, matching her syrupy tone word for word. "Don't worry, darling, he'll be here any moment."

Valerie giggled doubtfully and strode off to schmooze with the rest of the crowd. I was left with a feeling of smug satisfaction, dying to see the look on her face when Antonio and I hit the dance floor together.

If he ever gets here, I thought worriedly. A hollow feeling started in the middle of my chest, a cavernous fear that Antonio wasn't going to show. I struggled to fill the space with positive thoughts, promising myself that this homecoming would be better than the year before, with dopey Arnie. It would be romantic and wonderful and everything I'd hoped for. *It had to be.*

On stage, Dazzling Diamond Dave, a gyrating mass of hair grease, was doing a lame Elvis impersonation. The band plowed through a marathon medley of the King's greatest, without ever changing the tempo.

After thirty minutes of anxious waiting, I spotted Jordan wading through the crowd, heading in my direction. For the first time ever, I prayed he was on his way over to talk to me. I didn't think I could stand another minute alone.

My prayers were answered. Jordan came up beside me and handed me a cup of red punch. "This is for a terrific show."

"Thanks," I said, taking the cup gratefully. My mouth felt as if it were stuffed with cotton. "I had a great time."

"I could tell." He clinked his plastic cup against mine and took a sip. "You were really playing from the heart."

I blushed. "Is everyone still around?"

Jordan's dark eyes glossed over the crowd. He looked a million miles away. "Marissa and Buzz left to go see Smashing Pumpkins at the civic center," he said distractedly. "Andre went home—he was pretty beat. But I think Donny's around here somewhere, working the crowd." He turned and looked at me. "You know, I really like that dress."

"What if I told you it was made out of angora rabbit hair?" I said mischievously.

Jordan made a face. "I'd be completely sickened and disgusted."

"I'd like to see that," I said jokingly. "But unfortunately, the truth is it's only made out of cotton."

"Good," Jordan answered. "It looks so great on you, I'd hate to make you throw it away."

"I'm sorry, Jordan, but you couldn't make me do anything," I said with a rueful smile.

Jordan ran his fingers through his soft blond hair. "I can be very persuasive, Becky."

"Persuasive, no. Sneaky, yes."

"*Sneaky?*" he repeated.

I nodded. "Why didn't you tell me you play the sax?"

Jordan shrugged. "Because I don't."

"It sure sounded like you knew how to play in rehearsal the other day," I pressed.

Jordan finished off the last of his punch. "My dad has all kinds of instruments hanging around the house," he said casually. "Once in a while I'll pick one up and play around a bit. But my real specialty is the guitar."

"Oh, yeah?" I said, more impressed than I was willing to let on. "Why don't you play onstage?"

Jordan frowned. "Performing isn't my thing. It scares me to death."

Dazzling Diamond Dave and the Gem Tones were bouncing around the stage in their silver sequined jackets, looking totally ridiculous. The band was going at full tilt, the speakers blaring. I moved in closer to Jordan so he could hear me. "It's really not that tough. And it's a lot of fun."

"I don't think I could do what you do," Jordan said into my ear. "'Masquerade' was beautiful."

I turned my head and spoke into his ear. "You mean I didn't honk my way through it?"

"It must've been your lucky night," Jordan

134

teased. His warm breath tickled my ear. "I hope your boyfriend liked it."

I scanned the crowd for the hundredth time, but there was still no sign of Antonio.

"He hasn't shown up yet," I said, my mouth accidentally grazing Jordan's earlobe.

"I'm waiting for someone too," Jordan said. "She's late."

Diamond Dave pulled a silver handkerchief from his pocket and wiped his greasy brow. "Now we're gonna take things slo-o-o-o-w," he purred into the mike. The band came to a screeching halt as Dave began to sing "Loving You."

"I love this song," Jordan said, humming along with the words.

I turned my head to say something, and at the exact same moment Jordan leaned over to talk to me. We were staring face-to-face, my lips nearly brushing his.

Jordan held out his hand to me. "Would you like to dance?"

My eyes darted from the packed dance floor to the entrance of the gym. Antonio was almost an hour late. *He's not coming,* a voice whispered in the back of my mind. As the hollow space inside my chest kept growing, my hopes were diminishing.

"Wh-What about your friend—the, uh, the one you're waiting for?" I stammered.

Jordan sighed, looking around. "I still don't see her," he said. "Besides, one little dance won't hurt."

I put down my punch. I couldn't let the night slip by without dancing at least once. "All right," I said, taking his hand. "You lead the way."

Jordan weaved through the dancing couples, with me trailing behind, until we found an empty spot on the dance floor. In one smooth motion he curved his arm around my waist and pulled me close. The fingers of my right hand held gently on to his left while my other hand rested on his shoulder. My body felt stiff as we started to dance, my feet constantly bumping into his.

"I'm sorry—I'm not very good at this," I apologized, staring down at my awkward feet.

"Don't look down," Jordan said as we continued to sway. "It's easier if you keep your head up."

I lifted my head and looked up at him. His dark eyes were gazing down at me. "Like this?" I asked, moving stiffly.

"You're getting there," he said, his full lips curving in a slight smile. "But you have to relax a little."

I took a deep breath and relaxed my shoulders. My moist palm felt slippery in his hand. I let go for a minute and rubbed my damp hand against the side of my dress.

"Are you okay?" he asked.

I nodded. "I'm fine."

Where are you, Antonio? I thought sadly as we danced. It was supposed to be such a romantic night, but nothing was going as I had planned. I wanted to believe there was a good excuse for his not being there, but the cold sting of rejection was seeping deep into my bones.

I moved a little to the left, my foot accidentally stepping on Jordan's. "I'm so sorry!"

"It's all right," he said, his face twisting in a painful grimace. "But only one of us can lead."

"You lead," I said. "You know what you're doing."

Jordan's fingers tightened around mine. "If I lead, you're going to have to relax and learn to trust me," he said. "Do you think you can do that?"

"I'll try," I said. My head felt light, and a feeling of giddiness swept over me. I didn't know whether to laugh hysterically or burst into tears.

Without warning, Jordan spun the both of us in a circle. I resisted, my feet becoming entangled with his.

"You're fighting me," he said softly.

"So what else is new?" I answered.

He smiled at me, and I could feel the warmth of his hand on my back through the material of my dress. "Do you want to try it again?"

"Okay," I said, my pulse quickening.

Jordan turned, and I followed, letting my body go slightly limp. We spun perfectly in a clean, tight circle. I rested my arm across the back of his shoulders, holding on for dear life.

"That was great!" Jordan said, breaking into a brilliant smile. "Do you want to learn a different move?"

Before I had a chance to answer, Jordan gave me a gentle push so that I twirled away from him. My dress swirled dramatically as I turned. I was getting the hang of it. Then, still connected by our hands, Jordan pulled me back. I twirled toward him, coming to a stop in his arms. He held me close, our bodies pressed against each other.

"Where did you learn to dance like that?" I asked, staring deeply into his brown eyes.

"I don't know, Rebecca," Jordan answered thickly. He let go of my hand and wrapped both arms around me.

Without thinking, I drew my hands up, lacing my fingers behind his neck. I didn't know if the band was still playing—all I could hear was the pounding of my heart.

I can't believe this is happening, I thought.

Jordan lowered his head, his bristled cheek touching lightly against mine. I closed my eyes, feeling the damp heat rising from his skin, breathing in his musky scent.

A shiver ran through my entire body. I leaned my head against Jordan's. He held me tighter, humming along to the music. His soft voice filled my ears.

Then, very lightly, I felt Jordan's fingers stroking my back. My heart hammered against my rib cage, anticipating his every move. I turned my head, my mouth tracing a whispery trail from his ear along his jaw to his chin.

Jordan responded, tilting his head down until our lips met. I became lost in the moment, unaware of anyone around us. The emptiness I had been feeling earlier was filled with the warmth of the soft, slow kiss. A sense of completeness overwhelmed me, as though I had found some mystical treasure I'd been seeking for a long time without ever having realized it had been with me all along.

Jordan pulled away slightly. "I'm so glad my friend didn't make it," he said, rubbing his cheek against my hair.

"Who is she?" I asked softly.

Jordan kissed my forehead. "She calls herself Lavender."

An electric tingle shot through my spine. "Lavender?"

"That's not her real name," he said with an embarrassed laugh. "It's a long story, but basically I met her on the computer—"

I dropped my arms. *"Carlos?"*

Jordan froze for a second, then his eyes narrowed. "Don't tell me you're . . ." Then he started to laugh.

Jordan can't be Carlos! My mind struggled to comprehend what was happening. *How could I have been so wrong?* I wrestled myself free from his embrace. "You didn't know it was me?"

Jordan shook his head. "No clue," he said, brushing a strand of hair out of my face.

There were too many clues that pointed to Antonio, I reasoned. *Too many things that fit.* I couldn't have put all of those ideas in my head—unless someone had put them there for me.

I folded my arms across my chest. "You found out that I liked Antonio, didn't you?" A lump formed in my throat. I stared at him through blurry eyes.

Jordan pulled me off the dance floor. "Antonio?"

"You thought it would be funny to lead me on, to make me think I was writing to Antonio, when all along it was you I was writing to."

Jordan stared hard at me. "You thought you were writing to Antonio?"

"Don't pretend you didn't plan it that way!" I shouted, drawing more than a few stares from the couples around us. "You just love making fun of me!"

"Rebecca, I don't know what you're talking about. . . ." Jordan's voice trailed off.

"Yes, you do," I answered, the tears flowing

down my cheeks. I felt as if the entire world were collapsing around me. Nothing was as it seemed. "You destroyed one of the most important nights of my life. I hope you're happy."

Jordan held my elbows firmly. "Rebecca, if you want, we can go somewhere to talk about this—"

"Just leave me alone!" Yanking myself away from him, I backed off.

"Rebecca, wait!"

"I hate you, Jordan West!" I shouted as I whirled and ran toward the exit. "I hate you!"

Twelve

"I'M SO MAD, I could scream!" Leslie hollered the second I opened the front door on Sunday morning. Her skin was unusually pale, and her eyes were tinged with red from crying, just like mine. Obviously something big had happened.

I led her to the back porch. "What exactly did your parents say?" I asked. We sat down on the white wicker couch, where I had spent most of the morning remembering the horrible events of the night before.

Leslie's eyes welled up with tears. "They won't let me go to England," she began. "And to make matters worse, I'm not allowed to talk on-line with Edward anymore. Mom's getting rid of the on-line service today." She pulled a wad of tissues out of her pocket and blew her nose. "We really love each other, even if no one else believes it."

My heart went out to Leslie, but I was still

141

relieved that her parents had enough sense to stop her from making a huge mistake. I'd never dreamed it would be so easy to fall in love with someone through a computer, but it'd happened to both of us. "Leslie, what are you going to do?"

She shoved the wad of tissues back into her pocket. "I've been trying to get in touch with Edward, so he doesn't think I'm suddenly blowing him off."

"Did he give you his phone number?"

"No," she said, wiping away a tear. "But I know his dad's name. I managed to get the number through the international operator. Edward wasn't home, but I talked to his dad. He seemed really nice."

I suddenly felt terrible for Leslie. It seemed as though Edward might be a normal human being after all. What if she was missing out on the love of her life?

"Is Edward going to call you back?" I asked.

Leslie nodded. "But probably not right away—he went away with some friends for a few days. I'm sure he'll call as soon as he gets in."

"And then what?"

"That depends on Edward," Leslie answered. "If he says the word, I'm out of here. My bags are already packed."

My eyes burned, but no tears came. I wanted to beg Leslie not to leave, but I was afraid I might just end up driving her away. "How long do you think you'll stay?"

Leslie shrugged. "Maybe a week, maybe forever—it depends on a lot of things. I'd like to stay abroad for a while, though, just to show my parents I can do it." Her eyes watered as she said it. I knew she would miss her family a lot. She stood up. "I've got to go—in case he calls."

I grabbed on to her arm, the way she'd always grabbed mine. "Leslie, promise me you won't take off without saying good-bye, okay? At least give me a call so I know where to reach you."

Leslie gave me a big hug. "I promise." She pulled a piece of paper out of her pocket. "I don't know if you want this, but I printed it out before my mom disconnected the computer. It's a letter from Jordan—he sent it this morning."

I hesitated for a moment, my heart pounding in my throat.

Leslie handed me the letter. "At least read it. The guy sounds pretty upset."

After she left I sat on the couch staring numbly at the folded piece of paper in my hand. Finally, after a long time had passed, I decided to read what he had to say.

Date: Sun 8:30
To: Rebecca
From: Jordan
Re: Last night

> *Dear Rebecca,*
> *We need to talk.*
> *I'm not quite sure what happened last night, and I would love for you to explain it to me. Weren't we having a great time together? I've replayed everything over and over again in my mind but can't quite figure out what went wrong. Was it the kiss? If I*

did anything wrong, please let me know.

I still don't understand why you were so upset about my being Carlos. You've got to believe that I meant everything I ever wrote to you. I've been nothing but honest from the start.

Rebecca, I feel terrible—like I've done something wrong, but I don't know what it is. Let's get together tomorrow so we can clear the air.

Love,
Jordan

(P.S. I want you to know that before things turned bad, I was having an incredible time.)

There were too many confusing thoughts and feelings scattered in my mind and heart. I couldn't make sense of it all. It had felt so wonderful to be dancing in Jordan's strong arms, feeling his warm lips touching mine . . . but how could I know if he was telling the truth? I still had so many suspicions. Now that I was gaining a foothold in the band again, Jordan might have thought up the scheme to get me out once and for all. Or maybe it was just his way of getting back at me for having given him such a hard time. I wanted to believe he was telling me the truth, but I couldn't risk being hurt.

There's only one thing I can do, I thought as fresh tears came to my eyes. I picked up the letter, and in a sudden rush of frustration I tore it into a million tiny pieces. *I never want to see you again.*

"Please don't make me go out there," I begged Leslie on Monday morning. I was terrified of running into both Jordan and Antonio, and the girls' bathroom seemed like the only safe place in the entire school.

Leslie pulled her hair back in a silver barrette. "You can't stay in here forever."

"Oh, yes, I can," I said with determination.

Leslie's reflection frowned at me. "What an exciting life you're going to have, trapped in the girls' bathroom of Westfield High."

I rolled up the sleeves of my oversized white oxford and shoved my hands in the front pockets of my jeans. "You're right, it would be boring to stay in here," I said. "Maybe I'll just move to Mexico and assume a new identity."

"That's a start." Leslie nodded with approval. "At least they've got beaches." She handed me her pot of kiwi lip gloss. "Seriously, Rebecca, you're going to have to talk to Jordan and Antonio one of these days."

I dabbed the gloss on my lips. "I don't plan on it," I said. "Especially not Jordan—not after what he did to me."

Leslie turned to me, leaning her back against the wall. "Has it ever occurred to you that maybe Jordan isn't really a loser after all? Maybe the whole E-mail thing was an amazing coincidence."

"Not a chance," I answered, inspecting my lips in the mirror.

"But he seems like a really nice guy, and I always thought he had a thing for you," Leslie said.

I shook my head. "For some reason everyone thinks Jordan is such a great guy. Well, let me tell you something—he isn't. He's a completely insincere manipulator who does whatever he has to do in order to get people on his side."

"But he didn't get you on his side," Leslie countered.

"That's because I can see right through him," I said, handing her back the lip gloss. "And he knows it. That's why he was always trying to challenge me or embarrass me—it was all a big game."

Leslie's green eyes clouded. "Maybe you're right—but he's working for the band. You'll have to talk to him at some point."

"Only if I absolutely have to," I said firmly.

A sly smile crept across Leslie's face. "Talk about determination," she said. "So where does that leave Antonio?"

I slumped against the wall and groaned. "I'll have no trouble avoiding him—he probably can't stand the sight of me. I was so positive it was him, Les, that I made an absolute idiot out of myself."

"I'm sure you think it was much worse than it really was," she said.

My stomach started to feel queasy again. "All those times I thought I saw passion in his eyes, he was probably thinking, 'Who *is* this strange girl?'"

The warning bell for homeroom sounded. "If it's any consolation, he'll be going back to Spain in the spring," Leslie said. She picked up the stack of books she'd balanced on the trash can. "Do you want me to walk you to homeroom?"

"No, thanks," I answered, resting my head against

the cold cement wall. "I'm going to stick around here until the bell rings. I don't care if I'm late."

"Suit yourself," Leslie said, heading for the door. "If you're still in here at lunchtime, post a note on the door and I'll bring you some food."

"Thanks," I said with a laugh.

The door closed behind her, and I sank to the floor, sitting cross-legged as I waited for the second bell to ring. I hated hiding out, living in constant fear of bumping into Jordan or Antonio. It was only a month and a half into the school year, and already I couldn't wait until summer.

After the second bell rang, I grabbed my books and walked out. The hall was almost empty, except for a few students who were scurrying to class. I smiled to myself, grateful that I'd be able to run to homeroom without any trauma.

But as I turned the corner to the junior wing, my heart caught in my throat.

Antonio was walking toward me. I played it cool, walking calmly toward Mr. Wilson's classroom with my eyes focused on the floor. It was strange to see Antonio. The sight of him still made my pulse race, but I couldn't get used to the fact that I didn't know anything about him. From Carlos's letters I had built this clear image in my mind of who he was, and then suddenly I'd discovered it was all wrong. I had no idea who he was, and he didn't know me, other than the fact that I was some weird girl who liked breathing down his neck.

"Hi, Rebecca," Antonio said as he passed by me. I looked up, startled that he had even spoken to me. "Hi," I said quietly as I walked on.

Antonio stopped. "I saw you play on Saturday night," he said. "You were very good."

I stopped and turned around. "Thanks," I said shyly. Already I could feel the heat rising to my face. "I didn't see you at the dance."

"I couldn't stay very long," he said. His dark eyes were fixed on me. "I left right after your band finished."

Why is he talking to me? I wondered. It was the first time Antonio had ever initiated a real conversation with me. *He can't think I'm that much of a loser, or he'd never talk to me.*

"I'm glad you liked it," I said with a slight smile.

Antonio looked down at the floor, then back at me. "May I ask you a question?"

Mr. Wilson came out in the hallway to close the door. "Come on, Rebecca," he said, his hand on the doorknob. "The bell rang three minutes ago."

Slowly I headed for the classroom. "What is it?" I asked urgently.

Antonio followed me to the door. "Would you like to go out with me tonight?"

My stomach did a complete somersault. "What?" I said, not believing what I had just heard.

"I thought we could go to a movie or something." A strand of silky black hair fell across his eyes, and his curvy lips turned up slightly. "What do you say, Rebecca?"

At the sound of my name, my knees felt as though they were about to buckle. I rested a hand against the wall for support. *Antonio wants to go out with me,* I thought with thrilling pleasure. "I'd love to," I said, trying to sound calm. "But I have rehearsal at Java Joe's after school."

Antonio smiled, moving closer to me until I was practically pinned against the wall. "When do you get out?"

"Around six," I said breathlessly.

"All right," Antonio said, backing away from me. "I'll see you then."

Thirteen

BEFORE REHEARSAL I ran over to Leslie's to change for my date with Antonio. She let me borrow the black miniskirt and motorcycle jacket I had worn a few weeks earlier. The plan was to knock the socks off Antonio and completely annoy Jordan, all at the same time.

But when rehearsal started, Jordan didn't say a word. We pretty much stayed out of each other's way until the middle of rehearsal, when I had to stop the band because the sound wasn't quite right. Instead of yelling at Jordan directly, I tried to enlist Donny's help.

"Tell Jordan to adjust the levels," I said casually.

Donny sighed. "Why don't you tell him yourself? He's only a few feet away."

"Please tell him for me," I begged. "And I'll put in a good word for you with Leslie."

Donny's face brightened. "Yo, Jordan," he shouted across the room. "Adjust the levels."

"I already did," Jordan answered. "I heard Rebecca the first time around."

I blew a few notes on the sax, pretending I hadn't heard him.

"He said he heard you," Donny repeated, leaning over his drum set.

I turned my back to Jordan. "I know. I heard him."

"I'm just trying to help." Donny pouted. "Are you still going to put in a good word for me?"

"Yes," I answered with a sigh.

Jordan flashed the overhead lights to get my attention. "You know, it's okay to talk to me, Rebecca. My hearing's pretty good."

My jaw tensed. *Leave me alone,* I thought. *Things will be just fine if we pretend nothing ever happened between us. It'll be even better if you stop talking to me altogether.*

Just then Joe came through the door, carrying a tray full of Italian cookies and a pitcher of water. "I've got some good news for you," he said, setting the tray down on a nearby table. "Why don't you guys come over here and take a five-minute break?"

We all gathered around the table, wondering what was up. I took a seat between Marissa and Andre so that Jordan couldn't sit next to me. He ended up standing behind my chair instead.

Joe poured himself a cup of water. "It looks like my Saturday night booking can't make it this week—the poet who was supposed to do a reading has severe laryngitis and isn't supposed to talk for at least a week. After hearing about what a great job you did at homecoming, I thought I'd give you guys a shot."

We were all completely bowled over. It took a few moments for the news to sink in, but when it finally did, we were ecstatic.

"That's awesome, Joe!" Donny said.

Buzz nodded. "Cool!"

"Thanks so much," I said. "We really appreciate it."

Joe smiled. "I'm glad to do it."

Jordan tapped my shoulder as if he wanted to say something to me, but I ignored him. "Rebecca," he said in my ear, his warm breath tickling my neck, "I want to talk to you."

"Leave me alone, Jordan," I said out loud. The rest of the band was still talking about the gig.

Jordan reached for my hand. "We need to talk now," he said gravely.

I pulled my hand away. "I have nothing to say to you."

"Give me five minutes," he pleaded. "Hear me out—and then I'll leave you alone."

Reluctantly I followed him. I was prepared to stand my ground, no matter what it took. "Make it quick," I said, avoiding his gaze.

Jordan took a deep breath. He ran his fingers anxiously through his hair. "What's going on with you? What's up with this?" he said, looking at the leather jacket.

I smiled to myself. "It's none of your business."

"Did you get the letter I sent you?"

"Yes," I said curtly.

"Why didn't you respond?" he asked, his voice sounding strained.

My eyes rolled to the ceiling. "I have nothing to say to you."

Jordan's brow was creased with worry lines. "You're wrong," he said, touching my elbow. "I think you have a lot to say. Go ahead—get it all out."

I lowered my eyes. "I've put the entire incident out of my mind," I said evenly, despite the intense churning in my stomach. "Don't flatter yourself by thinking I'm upset about it."

Jordan's face turned red. "Cut it out, Rebecca! Stop playing games—just be straight with me!"

"How ironic," I said in a sarcastic tone. "All I've ever wanted is for you to be straight with me—and now you expect me to do that for you."

"Since when have I not been straight with you?" he demanded.

"Since the very beginning—and it's not just with me. It's with everybody." My insides felt as though they were being squeezed by a giant fist. "You came strolling in on that first day, the day Joe hired you, as if you owned the place. You were only supposed to take care of the sound for us, but suddenly you became buddy-buddy with everyone, trying to worm your way into the band. Everyone thought you were such a nice guy, but I knew you had ulterior motives."

"What motives?" Jordan said through gritted teeth.

My breathing became quick and shallow. "You started taking over—turning the band against me, making decisions you had no authority to make—"

"I told you before," Jordan cut in, "I was only trying to help. I had no intention of replacing you."

"Yeah, right," I scoffed.

Fire flickered in Jordan's eyes. "Things weren't going well for the band when I came along, so I thought I'd try to help you out, like by giving you the list of clubs—which, by the way, you ended up throwing in the trash."

"I thought it was a joke," I said defensively.

"That's my point," he said. "You don't trust me at all."

"You are the world's biggest manipulator," I shouted. "Everyone thinks you're so terrific—but it's all a great big scam."

Jordan shook his head in disbelief. "I try to get along with people, and you're calling me a liar. Thanks a lot."

"It fits, doesn't it?" I said, fighting to maintain the harsh edge to my voice. My insides were being squeezed tighter and tighter. "What else would you call someone who sends E-mail that makes it seem as if he's someone else?"

"Everything I wrote was the truth," he insisted. "I never pretended to be anyone else."

A throbbing pain pounded at my temples. "Then it's just a coincidence that you picked a Spanish code name and talked about traveling through Europe?"

The veins in Jordan's neck bulged. "My parents and I went to Europe two summers ago, and Carlos is the name of my favorite guitar player—Carlos Santana," he said fiercely. "Do you believe me now?"

"Why should I?"

Jordan paused for a moment, the corners of his mouth twitching as though he were searching for the right words. "Because I love you," he said quietly.

The room seemed to be spinning around me. My mind was too cloudy to think straight. *He loves me?*

Joe came up to me, a look of concern on his face. "Someone's here to see you, Rebecca," he said.

I looked over Jordan's shoulder to see Antonio waiting by the door. He smiled and waved, but I didn't wave back. "Please tell him I'll be there in a minute," I said to Joe.

"Let's go somewhere to talk this out," Jordan pleaded. "I think we really need to clear the air once and for all."

"I can't," I said firmly. "I have a date."

Jordan whipped around and looked to see who was at the door. "With Antonio?"

"He asked me out today."

The light in Jordan's eyes seemed to fade, and his face took on a pained expression. "So you told him to come here to rub it in my face?"

I looked away. "It was easier for him to meet me here. I didn't know . . ." My voice trailed off.

"How I feel about you?" Jordan finished for me. "How could you not know? There's an undeniable chemistry between us."

My head was swimming. "Look, I can't deal with this right now. Antonio's waiting."

"You don't even know him," Jordan argued. "Don't you remember? All those letters you wrote were to me, not him. Are you going to stay here and sort things out with me, or are you going to take off with some guy you hardly know?"

Antonio was getting impatient. I felt like a rope that was being stretched to its breaking point. "I'm

155

not going to break off a date just because you want me to."

"Fine," Jordan said, his eyes growing cold. "I guess you made your choice, then."

"You made it easy," I said, glaring at him. Without saying another word, I turned and headed for the door.

"Let me get that for you," Antonio said, taking my saxophone case from me and putting it in the backseat of his black Acura.

"Nice car," I said, admiring the sleek, glossy finish. "Did you have it sent over from Spain?" I asked jokingly.

Antonio opened the door for me. "I don't have a car at home. This belongs to my host family."

I slipped into the cool leather interior. *This is just what I need to make me forget about Jordan,* I thought as Antonio started the engine.

"I'm not really in the mood to see a movie," he said, the dashboard lights casting a greenish glow on his face.

"Where should we go, then?" A nervous tingle gnawed at my stomach.

Antonio backed the car out of the parking space. "How about if we take a walk on the campus?"

"I don't think that's such a good idea," I answered. "My dad works there—I don't feel like running into him, if you know what I mean."

Antonio smiled at me. "Do you have any other ideas?"

"How about the ice cream shop? It's only two blocks away."

He shook his head. "It's too loud and bright there. How about someplace quiet . . . where we can talk?"

I thought for a moment. "We could go to my house."

Antonio took a right turn. "I'll just drive around for a while. Let me know if you see anything interesting," he said, as if he hadn't heard me.

Silence fell between us. I stared out the window, watching the darkened storefronts whiz by. *I can't believe I'm on a date with Antonio.* I looked over at him and blinked to see if he was real.

"Are you all right, Rebecca?" he asked in a sultry voice.

"Yeah," I said with a laugh. I flipped my hair over my shoulder. "I just can't believe I'm here."

We came to a stop sign, and Antonio took a left. "Why not?"

I smoothed down my miniskirt and folded my hands in my lap. "It's a long story—but basically I've had my eye on you since the day you arrived."

Antonio looked at me. "I know."

Blood rushed to my face. "I was pretty obvious, wasn't I?" I said weakly. "I'm so embarrassed."

"You shouldn't be embarrassed, Rebecca." He reached across the seat and touched my hand. "You're a beautiful and smart woman. You should go after whatever you want," he said in his heavy accent. "I think strong women are sexy."

Antonio's fingers felt warm and smooth in my hand. "Why did you ask me out?" I asked, suddenly feeling bold. "Aren't you seeing Valerie?"

"Are you cold?" he asked, letting go of my hand.

"I'm fine," I answered.

Even though the temperature was comfortable, Antonio turned the heater on, sending a burst of hot air in my direction. He touched my hand again, and this time his palm rested on my thigh.

"Valerie and I go out sometimes, but we see other people," Antonio said. "I wanted to ask you out the moment I saw you in our computer class, Rebecca."

"Really?" My face was burning up from the hot air, and tiny beads of sweat were forming on my upper lip.

Antonio nodded. "But I said to myself, 'This woman is too smart and too beautiful to go out with me.'"

"How funny—I was thinking the same thing about you." I gently pushed Antonio's hand aside and unzipped my leather jacket. I laid it on the seat between us, but Antonio instantly hoisted it and tossed it into the backseat.

"Why don't you come over here?" he said, patting the empty space. "I feel like you're so far away."

I looked at Antonio's perfect face. He was staring at me intently, his dark eyes traveling from the top of my head to my knees, then back again, as if he were trying to memorize every detail.

"Okay," I said, wiping away the sweat that was trickling down my neck. Anything to escape the hot air that was blowing in my face. I slid across the seat.

"Much better," he answered huskily, snaking his arm around my waist.

I cleared my throat nervously. "Are you sure you can drive like this?"

As if to prove he could, Antonio took another left, turning the steering wheel effortlessly with the heel of his hand. "No problem," he said. In the glare of the headlights, we could see the brown gravel of an unpaved road up ahead.

I shifted uncomfortably in my seat as Antonio pressed me close to him. The air was thick and suffocating. This date wasn't turning out to be anything like what I'd expected. "Tell me about Spain," I said lightly.

"There isn't much to tell," Antonio whispered in my ear. "What do you want to know?"

"Tell me about your family," I prompted, pulling away from Antonio's firm hold. The car started to vibrate as we came to the end of the pavement and drove onto the dirt road. The inside of the windows was covered with a film of white fog.

"I have a mother, a father, two older sisters, and a younger brother," Antonio said blandly. He leaned forward, wiping away a bit of fog with his fingertip. Instantly the spot fogged up again. "I can't drive like this," he said.

"If you turn on the air conditioner, it'll clear up," I said quickly, but Antonio was already pulling the car over to the side of the road.

"We will have to wait until it goes away," Antonio said, turning. "What were we just talking about?"

"Your family," I said, turning on the air-conditioning myself.

"That's right, my family." Antonio's hand slithered up and down my side. His eyes were glazed. "What was it that you wanted to know about my family?"

"Anything," I said, my body rigid. Instead of being thrilled by his touch, I was feeling mostly annoyed.

"I have some aunts and uncles, a few cousins . . ." His voice disappeared into the air as he pulled me closer to him.

I put my hands on his shoulders to push him away, but his mouth suddenly came crashing down on mine without warning. There was no tenderness in his kiss—only his harsh, persistent lips trying to pry mine open.

"What are you doing?" I shouted, yanking myself free.

Antonio stared at me, his eyes wide open. "What's wrong, Rebecca?"

I straightened my shirt and grabbed the leather jacket from the backseat. "You've got the wrong idea about me," I said, putting the jacket on. "And I certainly had the wrong idea about you."

"What? You don't like this place?" he asked, throwing his hands into the air.

I pulled my saxophone case to the front seat and wedged it between us. "It looks like the fog is all gone," I said, staring at the windshield. "Time to take me home."

Fourteen

A S SOON AS I got home the phone rang. It was Leslie.

"Edward called," she said. Her voice wavered slightly, and I couldn't quite figure out what had happened. Fear surged inside me as I pictured Leslie at the airport, ready to board her plane.

"Where are you?" I demanded.

"Home," she said. "Don't panic—but can you come over right away?"

I got there in three minutes.

Leslie was sitting on her front steps, her face buried in her hands.

"What happened?" I asked, throwing my arms around her. "Edward doesn't want you to visit him?"

Leslie's voice broke. "He doesn't even know who I am."

"What do you mean, he doesn't know you?"

"He was so polite on the phone," Leslie explained, wiping the tears from her swollen eyes.

"He said, 'Miss Weaver, I'm afraid there's been a terrible mix-up.' Then he went on to tell me about a group of guys at the university who stole his password and assumed his identity on the Internet. It seems that the first conversation I had with Edward was real, but the rest of them were with a whole bunch of different guys." Leslie blew her nose. "I feel so cheap."

I'd had a gut feeling the situation would turn bad, but it was even stranger than I'd ever imagined. "What about the flowers, though?" I asked.

"Edward said that one of the guys in the group felt guilty about what they were doing, so he sent them to me."

I leaned my head against her shoulder. "You said Edward was nice—did you guys hit it off?"

"He's engaged," Leslie said. She started to giggle. "E-mail is so weird when you really think about it."

"Don't I know it," I said with a groan.

Leslie rested her head against mine as we watched car headlights zoom past us on the dark road in front of her house. "At least it worked out for one of us," she sniffled.

"It worked out just great," I said sarcastically.

"But it *did* work out for you," Leslie said, lifting her head. Her green eyes were wet with tears. "All you wanted was a romantic date for homecoming, and that's what you ended up with."

She was right. Dancing with Jordan had been the most romantic evening of my life. The way he'd held me gently in his arms, the soft touch of his lips, the earthy scent of his aftershave—all were imprinted in my memory. Even though things had gone bad toward the end, I knew I would remember that night forever.

Leslie dabbed her eyes with a tissue. "By the way, how did your date with the Latin lover go?"

"Don't ask," I answered heavily. "He was a total creep."

"I can't say I'm totally surprised."

I stared at her in disbelief. "Leslie! How can you say that when you were the one who encouraged me to go after him?"

"*You* wanted to go after him," she said matter-of-factly. "I was just being the supportive friend. If you'd asked me, I would've told you that Jordan is the man for you."

My disastrous date with Antonio had finally convinced me that no one could compare to Jordan. *Because I love you,* he'd said. No guy had ever said that to me before, and the memory of it washed over me like waves of liquid sunshine, seeping deep into my bones. But I also remembered all the horrible things I'd said to him during rehearsal. The warm feeling ebbed away, leaving me with a cold emptiness in the pit of my stomach.

"After the fight we had today, I doubt he's interested in me anymore," I said tiredly.

Leslie looped her arm in mine. "I'm sure he is—you guys were meant to be together. People can't just turn their feelings off like a light switch."

"It's not like this is the only time I've made him mad. I've given him a hard time from the very first day we met," I said, tears streaming down my cheeks. "I might as well face it—the guy of my dreams was right in front of me the whole time, and I blew it big time!"

Instead of rehearsing on Friday, the band decided to take the afternoon off to relax, have fun, and bond before our Java Joe's gig the following day. It had been a long time since we had done anything together as a band, and we were all looking forward to it. I was hoping it would give me a chance to make up with Jordan.

"Is everyone all set?" Jordan called as we piled into his parents' blue minivan.

Despite the cold weather, Donny, Andre, and Buzz were bent on going in-line skating one last time before winter descended upon us. They loaded the van with skating equipment, hockey sticks, a tennis ball, and two makeshift goals for a game of hockey. Since I was the only one who didn't have skates, we stopped at a sporting goods store so I could rent a pair.

"It's so cold!" Marissa said, blowing on her fingers to warm them. "Maybe this wasn't such a great idea."

"The cold is good for you," Buzz said, climbing into the van. "It clears your head. It's just what we need to improve our performance."

I loaded my skates, pads, helmet, scarf, gloves, and red parka into the back of the van. I was hoping to get the front seat next to Jordan, but Donny beat me to it.

"Hey, Donny," I whispered as Jordan slammed the back door shut. "Do you mind if we trade seats?"

"Where are you sitting?" he asked, turning around.

"Next to Andre, in the back," I said quickly. Jordan walked around to the driver's side.

Donny turned around to check it out, carefully weighing the decision. *Hurry up,* I thought with annoyance. *Doesn't he understand that I want to sit with Jordan?*

"I don't think so," Donny said, making a face. "There's too much stuff back there—it looks cramped."

Jordan opened the driver's–side door. "Thanks a lot," I muttered, climbing in the back.

"You can sit here on the way back if you want," Donny offered.

"Close the door!" Andre shouted, his teeth chattering. "I'm freezing."

Buzz paused for a moment, his hand resting on the inside door handle. "You know what they say—one must suffer for art."

"Who cares? Just shut the stupid door," Andre answered.

Marissa frowned. "I don't want to suffer. All I want is a cup of hot chocolate."

"We'll get some afterward," Jordan promised, revving the engine. "Joe gave me forty bucks— early payment for the gig—to take us all out to eat."

While everyone debated where we should go to eat, I stared out the window, pressing my face against the cold glass. Even though Halloween was still a week away, it already looked like snow. The clouds were a dark, puffy gray, sailing past us at twice their normal speed. The wind came up, rocking the skeletal tree branches back and forth.

"I vote for pizza!" Donny said, raising his hand.

Andre shook his head. "We had that last time. How about burritos?"

Jordan was unusually quiet. I watched his reflection in the narrow strip of rearview mirror above his head. I could only see his eyes and his forehead. His brow was furrowed. *What's he thinking about?* I wondered silently. *Is he thinking about me?*

"Come on, guys, we've got forty bucks!" Buzz cried. "We could have a real feast. Let's go to a nice Italian restaurant or something."

Donny nodded. "Then I could have pizza."

Jordan looked in the mirror, and our eyes locked for a moment. I watched as the crease in his brow deepened, then he looked away.

The van crossed the bridge over the Androscoggin River, then took an immediate left onto a narrow road. At the end of the road was an abandoned paper mill with an enormous paved parking lot.

Donny cupped his hands over his mouth like a megaphone. "Ladies and gentlemen . . . we have just entered skating paradise!"

I zipped up my parka and wrapped the scarf around my neck. Jordan parked the van next to the side of the building and we all tumbled out, along with our pile of equipment. Buzz and Andre set up the hockey goals while the rest of us put on our gear.

Marissa shivered as she slid the knee pads over her jeans. "We're going to die of hypothermia—all in the name of bonding," she said miserably.

"Stop complaining. You'll warm up as soon as you start skating," Donny said.

Buzz and Andre skipped the pads and put on

their skates. They grabbed hockey sticks and started shooting the ball back and forth.

I took a seat on the freezing cold cement steps and stared down at the pile of knee and elbow pads. Jordan sat down next to me and adjusted the buckles on his skates. "What do I do with all this stuff?" I asked.

"You put it on," he said flatly, without looking at me. "You've never been skating before?"

"No," I answered, picking up a pad. Donny stood up and skated over to where Buzz and Andre were playing around. Out of the corner of my eye I watched Jordan put on his gear, so I wouldn't seem so clueless. Taking the pad I was holding, I slipped my foot through it and tried to slide it up my leg.

Jordan snapped the buckle tight. "You're going to be a little shaky at first, but the most important thing is to be relaxed."

The pad stopped in the middle of my calf, and no matter how hard I tugged, I couldn't get it to go any higher. I glanced down at the tag—it was a medium. *This can't be too small for me,* I thought with embarrassment. *Am I really that fat?* I tugged again, determined to force it up to my knee, but it wouldn't budge.

Jordan looked over at me. "That's an elbow pad," he said with complete seriousness. He spoke to me as if I were some stranger he'd just met in the park.

"Oh," I said with a little laugh, though I was sure I could feel my heart crack in two. *He doesn't love me anymore,* I thought sadly. I wanted to tell Jordan how wrong I had been, but none of it seemed to matter. It was already too late.

I pulled the elbow pad off and slid a knee pad on

with ease. Jordan stood up and started skating in circles around the steps as I finished putting my gear on.

"Don't forget your helmet," he reminded.

"Right," I said, putting it on. I looked out across the lot to where everyone else was. Buzz and Donny were laughing up a storm, chasing each other around. Marissa was off in the corner by herself, practicing skating backward. "I'll never be able to do that," I said as I tried to stand up, holding on to the railing for dear life.

"Just take it easy," Jordan said, offering his arm for support. The gesture was more like a brother's than that of a potential boyfriend. "Do you think you can stand up by yourself?"

My ankles wobbled, and I lifted my arms slightly to gain balance. "I'm fine," I said coolly.

"Good," Jordan said with a firm nod. He spun around and tore down the lot at full speed, as if he couldn't get far enough away from me.

Now what? I thought, wobbling alone by the steps. Everyone else seemed to be having a great time way at the other end of the lot. Although it was only a few hundred feet away, it felt like miles. Jordan turned and skated backward, making graceful curves as he moved. His blond hair blew softly in the breeze as he skated, not bothering to look in my direction even once. He skated on, moving farther and farther away from me.

I strapped on my wrist guards with determination. "You can't run away from me, Jordan," I said into the chilly wind. "I'm coming for you."

And with that, I slid my right foot forward. My arms flailed as I struggled to maintain my balance.

My left foot followed stiffly. My body felt as if it were made up of all knees and elbows—angles jutting out in every direction. The helmet weighed down my head, and I felt like a little schoolkid with an overprotective mom. *Don't be afraid,* I told myself as I inched forward. *There's no way you can get hurt with this much padding.*

"We're starting the game, Rebecca," Andre called, holding up a hockey stick. "Whenever you're ready."

"I'll be right there," I shouted across the vast lot. Arms outstretched, I rolled myself in their direction inch by frightening inch. "I think I'm getting the hang of it," I said with a smile.

"Bend your knees and push off," Donny coached. "Take nice, easy strides."

I bent my knees a fraction and leaned forward. My stride was a little longer and a little smoother the second time. I tried it again, every ounce of my being concentrating on not falling. *I'm coming, Jordan,* I thought as I aimed straight for him.

"What a fast learner!" Andre said. "Keep it up, Rebecca!"

I leaned forward, and suddenly my wheels started rolling faster. Without even realizing it, I had hit a small incline, and even though it wasn't very steep, I was gaining speed at a frightening rate. "Oh, no!" I squealed as I coasted out of control. "How do I stop?" I shouted.

"Lean back on your heel!" Buzz shouted.

I lifted the toe of my skate, but it made me too unsteady, so I dropped it back down again. Sweat trickled down the side of my face. I was rolling faster and faster. "Watch out!" I screamed.

Jordan stood in place, watching me fly toward him. To the right of him was a big metal Dumpster. My body ached, imagining what it would be like to hit it. *I'm so glad I'm wearing my helmet,* I thought in panic.

Instead of letting myself be stopped by the Dumpster, I steered toward something much more pleasant—Jordan. "Oh, no!" I yelled, holding my arms out in front of me to soften the blow. I'd expected Jordan to jump to the side, but he stood right where he was, holding his arms out for me. Finally I crashed into him and held on for dear life.

"Thanks for stopping me," I said breathlessly, leaning against him for support.

"Learning how to stop is lesson one," he said, with a bit more warmth than before. He pushed a strand of light brown hair out of my eyes. "I think you're getting ahead of yourself."

"She made it!" Donny said. The rest of the gang applauded. I wanted to take a bow but was afraid of landing flat on my face.

Buzz whistled. "Good show!" he shouted. "But I bet you can't do this." Buzz skated at full speed toward an overturned garbage can and jumped high into the air, sailing over it. As he started to land he lost his balance and rolled to one side. He stuck his arm out to break his fall, his body twisting as he landed.

"Buzz!" Marissa screamed, hurrying over to him.

Buzz howled in pain. Jordan skated over, towing me with him. "Are you okay?" he asked.

Buzz grimaced, his face red. I looked down at

his arm, which was bent at an unnatural angle. Suddenly I felt nauseous.

"I think I broke it," he moaned.

"I'll go get the car," Jordan said, racing off to the end of the lot.

Andre and Donny sat Buzz up, careful not to move his arm. Marissa started to cry.

I took my scarf off and made a sling. "We'll get you to the hospital right away," I said. "Jordan's getting the van right now."

Buzz's breathing was heavy. "Hurry up," he said, gritting his teeth. "It's killing me."

Jordan skated back to where we were. "I can't drive us," he said wearily.

"Why not?" Donny asked.

Deep worry lines creased Jordan's forehead. "I locked the keys in the car."

"You *what*?" I shouted. "How could you do something so stupid?"

"You think I did it on purpose, Rebecca?" he asked angrily. "You really believe it's just another one of my nasty little pranks?"

"Don't you have an extra set of keys?" I asked in a panic.

"No," Jordan answered.

I rolled my eyes. "Nice going."

"Cut it out, you guys," Andre said. "Buzz is really hurting."

Jordan looked around. "Maybe I can find something to unlock the door with."

I unbuckled my skates as fast as I could. "While you attempt the impossible, I'm going to go down to the road to flag someone down."

"I'll go with you," Jordan said, following me to the cement steps. "You shouldn't go alone."

I put my sneakers on, not bothering to tie the laces. "Don't worry about me, Jordan," I said, heading toward the road. "I don't need your help."

Fifteen

"How's buzz?" I asked Donny when he came back out to the main waiting room. Donny sat down in the orange vinyl seat between me and Andre. "The doctor is putting on the cast right now," he said. "It was a good clean break, so he should heal completely."

"Did you see the X ray?" Andre asked, putting down the magazine he was reading.

Donny's eyes were big. "It was so cool. The bone was cracked right here. . . ." He pointed to the middle of his forearm.

"Okay, that's enough," I said, plugging my ears. "We really don't want to hear this."

"I think the doctor's letting him keep the pictures, so you can see for yourself," Donny said.

I made a face. "No, thanks."

"How long is he going to be in a cast?" Andre asked, his eyes glued to the television bolted high on the far wall.

"Six to eight weeks," Donny said.

"Oh, man," Andre groaned. "I don't mean to be a jerk or anything, but what about the band? What are we going to do without a guitar player?"

The thought had crossed my mind a thousand times on the way to the hospital. Just when things were starting to pick up for us, this had to happen.

"I guess I should call Joe and cancel tomorrow's gig," I said, trying not to sound disappointed.

"I think we should go on anyway," Andre said. "I told tons of people to come—I don't want to bag on them."

Donny grinned. "I've given the situation some thought, and I think I've found the perfect solution," he said. "I think we should ask Jordan to play."

Andre rubbed his chin thoughtfully. "He plays pretty well—plus he knows all our songs."

Donny nodded. "Then Buzz could do the sound board and lights," he said, looking around the waiting room. "By the way, where did Jordan go?"

"He went to get a cup of coffee," I answered. "But you can just forget about your idea. Jordan's totally afraid of playing onstage."

"He'll get over it," Donny said casually. "So are you going to ask him?"

A feeling of dread swept over me. "Do I have to?"

"You're the leader of the band, aren't you?" Donny asked.

I sighed. "I guess I am."

"Then it's up to you to ask." Donny winked at me. "I know you'll do a good job."

I trudged down the hallway toward the hospital cafeteria, my feet feeling like lead weights. Two hours before, I'd told Jordan I didn't need him, and suddenly there I was, ready to beg for his help. It was so humiliating.

Jordan was sitting by himself at one of the cafeteria tables, sipping from a paper cup full of coffee. He seemed lost in thought, a look of sadness on his face. I felt a pang of remorse in my heart, and I was so sorry for all the horrible things I had said to him. I wanted to kiss him, to tell him how badly I felt, to tell him I loved him.

"Hi, Jordan." I sat down in the chair across from him. "Did you get in touch with your dad?"

Jordan nodded, looking up from his coffee. His dark eyes seemed weary. "He has an extra set of keys at home, so we'll go over and get the minivan later."

I folded my arms and leaned my elbows on the table. "Buzz is okay, but he's going to have to be in a cast for six to eight weeks."

"Poor guy," Jordan said. He took a sip of coffee.

"Yeah, it's really too bad," I answered awkwardly. "And it's too bad for us—we don't have a guitar player now."

I'd dropped the hint, but Jordan didn't pick it up. "I guess you'll just have to play without one."

"We all agreed that it wouldn't sound very good," I said carefully. "You wouldn't happen to know anyone who could learn all of our songs by tomorrow, would you?"

Jordan tapped his fingers thoughtfully on the tabletop. "I do know a guy, but he's a manipulative, controlling creep who likes to play mean pranks on people," he said. "Believe me, he's not your man."

Impulsively I reached across the table and

touched his hand. "Yes, he is," I said thickly. "And I think the band would be incredibly disappointed if he didn't play for us."

Jordan pulled his hand away. "And how would you feel?"

"Devastated," I answered.

Jordan fell silent for a moment. "You could always ask your boyfriend, Antonio, to play for you," he said bitterly. "He's perfect."

"I was totally wrong about him. I was wrong about a lot of things."

Jordan drained the last bit of his coffee. "You said you didn't need me."

"I-I didn't mean it," I stammered. "I was upset about Buzz being hurt, that's all." I looked deep into his eyes. He seemed so far away. "I made such a big mistake, and I understand why you're so angry with me. I'm sorry. I know I blew my chance with you, and I regret it, but don't take it out on the band. We really need you."

Jordan stood up and put on his coat. "You hurt me so badly by going out with Antonio," he said quietly.

I held on to his sleeve. My eyes filled with tears. "What can I do to make it up to you?"

"I don't know if you can, Rebecca," he said tiredly. "I'm not sure it's even worth it." Gently he pulled his arm away. "I'm going to go now. I just want to sit and think for a while. Say good-bye to Buzz for me."

I nodded without saying a word, letting the tears roll down my cheek.

★   ★   ★

By the time Saturday night rolled around, we still had no idea whether Jordan would play guitar for us, but we all decided to go on with the show anyway. Every nerve in my body was on edge, waiting to hear from him. I was riding a roller coaster of emotion—one minute feeling confident that he would show up, the next minute terrified that he'd never speak to me again.

Twenty minutes before the show, I was frantic. "Have you heard from Jordan?" I shouted at everyone who passed by.

Donny shook his head.

"Not since the last time you asked me—five minutes ago," Buzz answered. Not even Joe had talked to him.

I popped a reed into my mouth and took a deep breath, hoping the prickly anxiety that was slithering up my back would disappear.

"I hate to ruin your night," Leslie said, scurrying over to where I was standing, "but guess who just walked in the door."

I took the reed out of my mouth. "Jordan showed up," I said with a heavy sigh of relief. I craned my neck to look, but the speakers were in my way.

"No," Leslie said, gripping my arm. "Antonio . . . and Valerie."

My heart sank. "Who cares?" I said with a frown.

"I can't believe this," Leslie said, making a face. "They're making out in a public area—how tacky."

"They're made for each other." I adjusted my neck strap.

Donny came in carrying a snare drum. "Still no Jordan?"

"Not yet," I answered.

"Hey there, Leslie," Donny said with a shy smile. He self-consciously smoothed his hair, which he'd tamed with a bit of gel. "Glad you could make it."

"Nice hair, Donny," Leslie said.

Donny dropped the snare on his foot and made a great effort to conceal the pain he was clearly feeling. "You think so?" he squeaked.

Leslie nodded. Her lips curved in a flirtatious smile. "I like it a lot."

"What a coincidence. I like your hair too," Donny answered. "Maybe we could go to the hairdresser's sometime and get a trim together."

Leslie laughed. "Maybe."

Just as I walked to the front of the stage to check the monitor, the side door opened. It was Jordan, and he was carrying a guitar case.

I put my sax down and ran over to him. "You made it!" I gushed. I lifted my arms to give him a hug, but then I hesitated and let them fall limply at my sides. "I'm so glad you came."

Jordan put down his guitar. "Is everything ready to roll?"

"Yeah," I said. "Are you?"

He nodded. "I'm playing cold, so don't expect much."

I bit my lip. "I won't."

Jordan took off his jacket and looked around, completely businesslike. "Did you write out the chords for me?"

"They're taped to your mike," I said.

For the first time in days, Jordan stared at me intently, as if he were trying to look inside my soul. "You knew I'd come?"

"I hoped," I admitted.

Jordan looked down at the floor. "Last night, when I was thinking about things, I kept coming to the same conclusion," he said softly. "I realized how much I missed you."

"I missed you too," I said, unable to hide my emotion. I reached out for Jordan and held him close, pressing my cheek against his warm chest. It was as if I had gone on a long, exhausting journey, and after nearly losing my way, I had finally made it home.

Jordan tenderly kissed the top of my head. "No more fighting, okay?"

"Okay," I said contentedly. "Not unless it's absolutely necessary."

"When would it be necessary?" he asked.

"I don't know," I said with a mischievous smile. "Say, if one of us accidentally locks the keys in the car."

"That would be a good reason," Jordan teased. "Or an even better reason would be if one of us throws away a list of jazz clubs that the other one has worked so hard to get."

I shook my head. "That's not a good reason."

"I have an even better reason not to fight," Jordan said, his eyes shining.

"What is it?" I asked coyly.

Without answering, Jordan tilted my head toward his, and then he kissed me.

Sixteen

"WE'RE ALMOST THERE," I said, bracing myself against the cold wind.

Once we reached the edge of the clearing, the trail became winding and narrow. It ended at the rocky base of a steep slope, where jagged slabs of granite formed a natural ladder to the top of Bradbury Mountain. Jordan climbed ahead, his strong arms giving me support on the tough spots.

When we finally reached the top, daylight was beginning to fade. "We made it just in time," Jordan said as we took a seat on the edge of the rock.

The raw and blustery wind swirled around us as we looked down at the bare branches of the trees. Overhead, clouds floated above us, but the sky was clear at the horizon. Something tickled my cheek, and I looked up to see feathery white flakes falling from the sky.

I held out my hand to catch a few. "It's snowing."

"You know," Jordan whispered in my ear, "of all the people I could've met on-line, I'm glad it was you."

"I'm glad it was me too." I closed my eyes, feeling the heat of Jordan's lips as they traveled from my ear down my neck.

"You're missing an incredible sunset," I said with a giggle, looking out over the miles and miles of horizon. Gold became crystal pink as it deepened into an electric tangerine sun.

Jordan nuzzled my neck. "Does it look as beautiful as we pictured on our imaginary date?"

"It's a million times better," I sighed. "It's the real thing."

Do you ever wonder about falling in love? About members of the opposite sex? Do you need a little friendly advice but have no one to turn to? Well, that's where we come in . . . Jenny and Jake. Send us those questions you're dying to ask, and we'll give you the straight scoop on life and love in the nineties.

DEAR JAKE

Q: *I've been dating two boys at the same time and they couldn't be more different. Peter is very shy, but cute and incredibly sweet. He writes me love notes all the time and he even wrote me a poem.*

Brian is outgoing and fun. He's a starter on the basketball team and he's one of the most popular guys in school. I know that both Peter and Brian like me a lot and neither one knows about the other. Here's my problem, Jake. I'm afraid that if I don't choose one of them, they'll each find out about the other and then they'll both dump me. Who should I choose?

NC, Fairfield, CT

A: It sounds as if you're enjoying playing the field right now. Brian and Peter are showering you with attention. Who wouldn't want to live it up? But be sure that you're open and honest in each relationship. Make it clear to both that while you enjoy dating them, you're not ready to make an exclusive commitment yet. Otherwise, you're right—you could end up losing them both.

And here's the tricky part. You might find, as you're reading my answer, that you were secretly hoping I'd advise you to go for Peter, or for Brian. Maybe the idea of continuing to date them both disappoints you, and you already know who really lights your fire. Be on the look-out for these kinds of feelings. Eventually, your heart will give you the answer you're seeking.

Q: *My boyfriend, James, constantly flirts with a girl in my class named Shelly, who rides the same school bus as he does. Every day, as soon as their bus pulls up to school, all my friends who were on the bus with them tell me that James and Shelly were all over each other for the entire ride. Meanwhile, if he even sees me talking with an-other boy, he gets upset. Once when I was talking to the guy I sit next to in math class, James threatened to break up with me because he thought we were flirting. Am I crazy or is this unfair?*

DW, Portland, TN

A: It's *completely* unfair of James to demand that you not have any guy friends, while he flirts with Shelly as much as he likes. Remember, though, that at this point you don't have the full story. All you know is what you've heard from your friends—and it sounds as if they might be exaggerating.

Tell James what people have been saying about him and Shelly. Ask him if he's been flirting with her, and tell him that hearing about this first thing every morn-ing is not the way you like to start off your day. Let him know that these stories hurt your feelings and that if they continue, your relationship with him will be hurt, too. Then let James take it from there. If he's concerned about your feelings, he'll want to put a stop to the rumors—and to the flirting. After all, he hated it when he thought you were flirting with that guy in math class. He should understand that the same kind of behavior that hurts him hurts you, too. If he's not willing to acknowledge this, you need to move on.

DEAR JENNY

Q: *I have a huge problem, Jenny. I'm totally into this guy in my class named Justin. I've been interested in him for about three years now. He once told me that he just wanted to be friends, and he broke my heart. But I never stopped caring for him.*

Now Justin's dating my best friend, Sarah. Whenever I see Justin with her, I wish he were with me instead. I can't help it—every day I like him more and more. Should I try to avoid Sarah when she's with Justin, or should I hang out with them both and pretend that nothing's wrong?

CM, Hollywood, FL

A: When you care deeply for someone who doesn't feel the same way about you, it can be very painful and difficult to let go. But the time has come for you to take that step. While Justin likes you as a friend, he has chosen to date Sarah. As much as that hurts, there's nothing you can do to change it.

Tell Sarah the truth— that you're glad she's found true love, but it's hard for you to be around her, since you have feelings for Justin. You and she can still spend time together, without Justin. And you should start looking for a love that will bring you all the warmth and happiness you deserve.

Q: *This past spring, I went out with a guy named Ian. He was really great at first, but after we'd been dating a few months he became abusive. He'd get angry at me for no reason and then he'd yell and push me around. He even hit me once. I broke it off in early June because I was afraid it would get worse.*

Since then I've been single and recovering. I've met some nice guys at school and am friends with them. The problem is that I don't trust anyone. Ian broke my trust when he abused me. I want to feel comfortable around my male friends, but I don't know if they're going to yell at me if I say the wrong things. I'm afraid they'll lose their tempers.

I really like one guy in particular—Josh. I feel that Josh is respectful and caring and would never hurt me, but I still have doubts. Please help!

KC, Minneapolis, MN

A: Once someone has betrayed you, it can take a long time to rebuild your self-confidence and to learn to have faith in people again. You've been through a terrible experience and now you need to let the wounds heal so that you can go on with your life as a stronger person. You've already done yourself the biggest favor you possibly could by getting out of the bad relationship. Don't rush into anything new until you feel ready. You may feel better if you talk about what happened with friends, family, or even a counselor, minister, or rabbi.

You're on the right track with Josh. Get to know him slowly. Let him prove to you that he can treat you with respect. Not all men are like your ex-boyfriend. There are some great guys out there, including the special one who will be lucky enough to win your love.

Do you have questions about love? Write to:

Jenny Burgess or Jake Korman
c/o Daniel Weiss Associates
33 West 17th Street
New York, NY 10011